A Nick and Sherry Story

Waterton Zoo

Carolyn Houghton

Elyse Wheeler

DANCING CROWS
PRESS

ISBN 13: 978-1-951543-08-2

Library of Congress Control Number: 2020912750

Cover art by Colin Wheeler, MFA, ABD
strickenbrow@gmail.com

Authors' photos by Keith May
mayphotoanddesign.com

DancingCrowsPress@gmail.com

Dedication

This work is dedicated to Celia Walsh and Colin Wheeler ... the brightest lights in our lives.

Acknowledgments

We would like to thank our dear friends, Ann Brock, Terry Pirch and David Weiner for being our beta readers. Their insightful comments and warm encouragement helped us improve our story and bring more life to our characters.

Thanks also to the members of the Carrollton Writers Guild, especially the Just Prose members (especially Stephanie Baldi), for thorough critique and providing the momentum to finish this story.

By the Authors

Foxhaven Chronicles

Raven's Eye (2019)

Wolf's Eye (coming in 2021)

The Cast

Sherry Ramhill: Lord and Lady Ramhill's third child, she earned her degree as Veterinarian Extraordinaire for Other Species in England.

Madam Miriam DeMarco: She is a pillar of Waterton Society and co-founder the Wise Women Circle and.

Professor Vincent Lizzard: The Professor is a seven-foot shape-changing lizard who is proficient in astronomy and alchemy among other disciplines.

Sir Nigel Ramhill: Sir Nigel is Sherry's great (how many greats is uncertain) uncle. He is currently studying alchemy and thaumaturgy having mastered the other arts.

Nicklas Szabo: Nick is a native of Waterton and the owner of the Waterline Bar. He inherited the bar from his father soon after his return from a tour of duty in the Navy.

Christian McMillan: Hailing from Scotland, Christian is Nick's sparring partner and fellow protector of the Midnight Crew.

Gino: Originally from Italy (in what century, no one knows), Gino is the talented and inspired bartender at the Waterline Bar.

Yancy Fairhaven: A native son, Yancy is the somewhat reluctant Mayor of Waterton. He'd rather be out on his Harley.

Triss Fairhaven: Triss is Yancy's wife who he met and married when he went traveling by motorcycle.

Jonas Bernstein: From New York City and fresh out of college, he is the administrative assistant to the Mayor.

Granny Kent: She is the purveyor of magickal items at Granny's Attic.

Letitia: She is a demon seeking refuge.

The Cat:

Miasma: Enigmatic cat, she enjoys teasing Sherry, hunting the garden pixies in a game of hide and squeak, and disappearing ala her favorite character in Alice in Wonderland.

The Pixie Clan:

Petri: He is the lead male of the pixies living in Madam's garden.

Maribelle: She is the lead female of the pixies and Petri's love interest. She isn't too sure about him, though.

The Wererat Clan:

Anastasia: She is the clan mother and its stabilizing force.

Marty: Married to Anastasia, Marty is the recognized clan leader.

Micah: Micah is the eldest son of Marty and Anastasia. He is the primary assistant at the Waterton Zoo.

Garnet: She is Marty and Anastasia's youngest child at seven years old.

Zoo Family:

Billy Boy: Billy Boy is the furriest resident at the Waterton Zoo. He is an American Bison who loves to have his head scratched.

Gula: Gula is a visiting wolverine.

Cuddles: He is an egg-loving python.

Badal: An Asian elephant who loves to push Micah into the mud.

The Gargoyle Clan:

Arnie: Arnie is a gargoyle from the St. Jude Catholic Church. While his family still resides on the roof, he is afraid of heights.

Chazel: She is Arnie's wife and the gargoyle clan spokeswoman.

The Troll Clan:

Madrecita: She is the Clan Mother and the inspired chef at the bar.

Gregariel: Greg is Madrecita's husband-partner and foreman of the Midnight Crew.

The City Council:

August Ambruson: August is a Council member and pharmacist in Waterton.

Cynthia Pierce: Cynthia is a Council member and town busybody.

Abigail Warren: Abigail is a Council Member.

Markus Whitmore: Markus is the Council Chairman and jeweler. He is the former mayor.

Santos Corporation:

Dawson Hughes: Dawson is the dashing and brash team leader from Santos Corporation.

Sam, Gene, Eric and Nate: They are team members.

Chapter One

Sherry meets Madam Miriam and tours the Zoo

Sherry Ramhill expected the Colonies to be a refreshing change from her home in England but her host's ramrod straight spine transported her back to the head mistress' office at Wycombe Abbey School (Young Ladies Only). And she was in trouble already.

Madam Miriam DeMarco sat in her wingback chair, the majestic Victorian house a fitting backdrop for her well coifed white hair and stern expression. Adjusting her shawl over her sapphire silk suit, she raised the pearl-handled letter opener and deftly applied it to the creme linen envelope.

"Sit down," she said. "Pour the tea. I assume you have retained your heritage to some small degree."

"Yes, Madam, I have."

"Good. Now, don't fidget."

Sherry worked to compose herself, wondering who on earth would have the nerve to fidget before this woman. *Charlie wouldn't be able to stop his fingers from drumming ... or his knees from jumping. Damian would be stupid enough to try and intimidate her. Bet she'd turn him into a frog—or worse, she would!* Sherry's mouth quirked up until she caught the fright's eyes studying her.

"I amuse you, Miss Ramhill?" Madam arched an eyebrow.

1

"Oh no, *no,* not at all, Madam. I was trying to collect my wits." *And avoid my mind running too fast for my mouth.*

"Or perhaps the other way around." Madam tapped the folded letter with a manicured nail. "According to your Aunt Agatha, you've been observed to lose those wits at the most inopportune times. Speaking out to the Interspecies Council regarding our other friends as cousins and equals is not a way to endear yourself to the paranoid power holders. You did yourself no favors."

Sherry sat forward, preparing to engage in her own defense.

"And," Madam continued, "worse, you've brought harm to those you say you care about by raising everyone's consciousness regarding our friends' abilities and desires. Your affair with Alred was simply not to be tolerated."

"Now see here, we were friends and I am not about to apologize to you or anyone else for caring for the poor Zombie. Losing his head all of the time." She set her teacup down, shook back her long brunette hair and stood up. "If you think you have the right to scold me, you are off your nut. I may have embarrassed my Aunt, but *I* am not embarrassed at all."

"Young woman." Madam's voice barely above a whisper, she brooked no further retort. "Sit down."

Sherry hesitated, her indignation locking her knees in place. She pulled down the hem of her green striped mohair suit jacket.

"I said, sit down. I am not scolding you. You would have no doubt in your mind if I took it upon myself to admonish you. If you wish to fall in love with the boxwood in my front lawn, it would not upset me in the least. But you were not mindful when you brought that community under unwarranted scrutiny. Shameful." She pointed to the half-finished cup of tea. "Finish your tea."

2

Sherry lowered herself into the chair and picked up the tea cup.

"Before I offer you the project — with which you may, perhaps, redeem yourself — I must be assured you have learned some discretion. You are *not* convincing me at this moment."

Sherry sank back onto the tapestry cushion. *Aunt Agatha would meet her match here*, she thought.

Indeed, she has many times in the past.

Sherry jumped, fumbling the china cup. Sensing eyes appraising her, she counted two breaths before she raised her head to find Madam engrossed in the documents before her.

Shrugging, she picked up a cookie from the tray. *Ah well, I may as well enjoy these lemon cookies. They are quite good.* Her mind wandered over the events which landed her in America rather than working as a veterinarian in Cambridge and living in her eccentric Uncle Nigel's cottage. *I would be under less scrutiny there. I shan't be pished and tuttuted at much longer.*

You're dropping crumbs on the Afsar carpet.

Sherry jumped, crumbling the last bite. She dusted it from her lap into her hand. Her cheeks burned from the unidentified correction. She glanced in Madam's direction but her eyes were still on the letter. Without moving her head, Sherry scanned the room, straining her peripheral vision until her head hurt.

Don't be a goose. Over by the window.

She turned toward the bay window overlooking the river. A large long-haired cat returned her stare.

You? You are speaking to me?

3

Well, it isn't the mouse. A thin, grey tail twitched from under the teacup-sized paw. *He isn't up to a conversation.*

Her pink tongue swept out to clean the ruff on her shoulder.

You do have the blood line to be hearing us. Even though you were thinking loudly rather than conversing properly.

Thank you ... I think. And I wasn't trying to have a conversation, rather musing on my own thoughts." Sherry studied the silver and black striped cat.

Do you charge me with eavesdropping? Her hindquarters twitched rapidly back and forth.

Sherry hurried on. *No not at all. It's just that, in the past, I had to focus very hard in order to have any ... internal ... communication with any ... being.*

The cat licked down her shoulder, the rear end motion ceasing.

You are a lovely cat. Sherry nodded in her direction.

Cat? The cat looked around, over her shoulder and under her paw. *Where?*

"If you two are through chattering, I require your attention." Madam's voice cut through Sherry's concentration.

Sherry strained to turn toward her hostess, but the cat drew her eyes and held her still. The mouse now dangled by its tail from white incisors. The cat leapt from the windowsill and sashayed from the room.

I require cream ... not milk. Salmon ... not tuna.

She faded from sight, the light stripes exiting last.

Sherry desperately tried to curtail her rising giggle which, upon inevitable escape, earned an echoed snort from the old woman. They each raised an eyebrow at the departure.

"Miasma is an impatient and demanding sort. However, her example is one to follow. We will stroll." Madam rose, walking briskly down the hall to the back door.

Sherry trailed behind. *I don't care to be the little lamb caught in this particular shepherdess' hook*, she thought.

Madam descended the back steps from the wrap-around porch.

Sherry's mouth dropped open. A lush garden stretched several hundred feet behind the house.

"Bliss. How could anything be lovelier? This is how I always imagined Eden would look." Sherry wandered along the crushed rock pathway, a beatific expression on her face. "It smells so delicious. Thyme and chamomile just cropping up along the ground ... so soft and comfortable."

Madam sat on a white marble bench, her eyes following her new charge.

A whirring noise distracted Sherry from her nose. She peered at the shivering leaves of a scarlet begonia. "Pixies? Cannot be. It is much too cold in this region." She looked for her hostess. "And there isn't any magic in the Colonies to attract them."

"Quite certain, are you?" Madam arched an eyebrow.

"Yes, quite." Sherry set both feet and squared her shoulders. "It is a fact clearly delineated in *Twhistler's Investigation into Magick Beyond the British Borders*. He is emphatic all magic stems from the original Britons as evidenced by Stonehenge." She fell into recitation from memory. "Magick's loss beyond the borders is due to the reduction in Merlins. When Merlins were in abundance and ..." She shifted her weight to her heels then rocked onto tiptoe. "When they worked in concert to balance the leylines … which wasn't often as they had such huge egos…"

Madam held her lace handkerchief to her lips, her shoulders shaking.

"Magick flowed from the source—Stonehenge, naturally—to all other continents. But it has drained away without the constant refreshing return flow."

"Are you quite done, my dear?" Madam asked.

Sherry blushed under the hawkish stare. Madam twitched her handkerchief in the air. She spoke four words, foreign to Sherry's ear, in a high-pitch. The begonias, dahlias and gerbera daisies rustled and swayed. Pixies flew into the air in a swarm and beelined for Sherry, tugging at her hair and pulling on her clothes.

"Ow. Stop that." She waved her hands shooing away the small creatures.

"No Magick in the Colonies, you say?" Madam pulled a toffee from her pocket and unwrapped the sweet treat keeping her fingers from the sticky surface.

Sherry turned in circles, her hair splayed out in all directions by the circling pixies. She implored them to stop. Finally, she slapped at one who pulled on her nostril. The small creature fell to the gravel path and lay still.

"I see you peeking at me. You do not fool me." She bent forward to check on the little male dressed in luxuriant green silk. The swarm acted in concert flying full tilt into her backside and tipping her onto the ground, her hands saving her from a nosedive into the grass.

"Now, quite enough!" She snarled as she righted herself.

"I would say it is." Madam held the toffee out on her open palm and uttered another high-pitched word. Two pixies broke away from the swarm hovering over Sherry. Between them, they lifted the toffee and flew erratically into the red begonia. Excited chittering diverted the remaining winged creatures. Silence descended on the garden.

Sherry rose and brushed fruitlessly at her sullied suit. She fought to keep the trembling from her voice. "Are they safe here?"

"They're quite safe … for the moment. If you are successful in your task, they will remain so. Down the path and through the hedge is the private entrance to Waterton Zoo."

Sherry strained on tiptoe to see the garden's end. The little male pixie zipped in and grabbed her hair. He wrapped himself in a lock, purring contentment. Sherry worked to disentangle him, unsuccessfully, while she tried to pay attention to Madam.

"You have not attended a single word." Madam rose, towering over her.

Sherry dropped her hands from her hair, shushing the laughing pixie. Madam's long fingers trapped the small creature. She unwrapped him, pulling the hair free from his tight grasp.

"Now, Petri, I do enjoy your shenanigans, but you must allow me to conduct necessary business. You promised to weed the foxglove." The pixie flew up to her shoulder and reached as far around her neck as his small arms allowed. He kissed her cheek then whirred away.

"You will pay attention. This is your last chance."

Sherry tried to find words to refute the decree but despair sapped her courage. *It is true.* Her chin fell onto her chest and she thought for a moment about collapsing on the ground in tears.

Warm fingers lifted her face. Madam's crystalline gaze pierced through her. Sherry took a deep breath.

7

"You have your Mother's good soul and Agatha's barbwire constitution. I see it in your eyes and in your carriage … when you aren't slumping." Madam dropped her hand and set off for the house. Her words swept back to Sherry. "There is much to do. You best get started."

Sherry straightened, rising on her toes to stare at the hedge line demarking the border with the zoo. Feeling Miasma's gaze, she peered along the daylilies.

Do what? Sherry asked. Madam disappear up the path. She glared at Madam's straight back. *She could have explained things more … given me specific guidance.* She stamped her foot. *Why do I care what she thinks?*

Because she really does hold your last chance and … Miasma streaked between her legs upsetting her tenuous balance. *She's decided to give it to you.*

Vertigo struck, her emotions in a whirl. Sherry sat abruptly on the path again.

She has?

Miasma leapt over her legs, chasing a lizard from the marble bench. The lizard disappeared into the sage border with Miasma just behind.

Sherry closed her eyes against tears. She took a deep breath inhaling the scent of sage and reveling in the warm sun on her face. The unshed tears under control, she stood, brushing the dirt and leaves on her skirt. "I stand corrected." She pulled her felted jacket cuffs back into place. "At least, I think I can stand."

"If you are ready, we can continue your tour."

Sherry startled, searching the path for Madam while registering the different and young voice. She jumped outright when a shadow in her peripheral vision grew from small to slightly above her height. He grabbed her elbow to steady her as her foot twisted on the rock edge.

"Thank you," she said. "Without you, I would have met the walk for the third time." She looked ahead on the path and then back toward the house but her hostess was nowhere in sight. Turning to the lad, she studied him.

Straight, brown hair shot through with blond covered his eyebrows and partially obscured his deep brown eyes which stared directly back into her own. He held out his hands on either side, palms up. The long fingers and narrow palms drew Sherry's eye. Dirt smudged the knuckles but his fingernails were immaculate.

"Who are you?" she asked.

"Micah." He smiled at her. She waited. He continued smiling

"And what is a Micah?" She tapped her foot, trying to regain her composure and predominance.

"Your guide." His eyes twinkled. "Come along, please. We haven't all day."

"All right then." She strode down the walk. "Just where are we going?"

"To the zoo." He turned to the right and disappeared into the hedge. Sherry stopped, skidding on the white pebbles. She studied the hedge finding no break in the eastern red cedar trees.

Okay, this is a game. She walked back along the line checking for scuffs in the gravel. *And I am good at games.* She followed the subtle ridge created by Micah's boot. *Here,* she thought. Pulling aside the branch, she scrunched down to duck under the next branch. Watching her footing, she crept through the hedge until she found grass again.

Straightening, she dusted down her skirt. Feeling she was being watched, she scanned for Miasma. Not finding even a hint of the cat's tail, looked up. Large black-brown eyes

9

fringed with two-inch long black lashes blinked at her. Silver dollar-sized nostrils blew hot air into her face.

She froze.

The massive, furry head tossed from side to side. Tearing her eyes away, she studied the expansive neck, shoulder, hump towering over her head. *Horns, sharp horns.* Another hot blast ruffled her collar. She reached up and stroked the soft forehead. The bison lowered his head, his tail swinging from side to side.

"Don't stop." Micah's voice came from just over her shoulder.

"But I have to … sometime." She turned toward the sound, her hands itching for Micah's neck. The muzzle nudged her shoulder, knocking her back into the cedars.

"Scratch." Micah suggested.

Sherry dug her fingers into the thick fur. The bison shuddered. His head sunk lower and lower until she scratched his ears. His deep huffing vibrated through her.

"You've made a friend." Micah held out a large barley sheaf. "This is Billy Boy." The long tongue curled around Micah's hand pulling the barley from his grip. Grinding filled her ears. Sherry ran her hand under the powerful jaw. Air exploded from his nostrils blowing barley seeds in Sherry's face.

Sherry tapped her French-finished fingernail on Billy Boy's nose. "Silly boy. Blow in my ear, and I will follow you anywhere."

Micah's exhale rivaled Billy Boy's.

Sherry turned on him. "What?"

"Nothing." He grinned and set off across the pasture. Opening the gate, he disappeared down the overgrown lane.

"Well." Sherry stamped her foot. Billy Boy startled, lumbering away into the tall grass. A wary eye on the swinging tail, she strolled from the pasture and latched the gate. *He is not going to lead me about on a leash. I've had about all the fun and games I can stand for one day.* A white pebbled concrete walkway stretched ahead, gently curving in and out cradling the various viewing positions. She took her time looking into each enclosure. The shrubbery and plantings were immaculate but she did not see many animals.

It is afternoon. I suppose everyone is taking a siesta. The signs indicated bongos, oryx, sitatunga. *Hooved herbivores,* Sherry classified them as she moved along. Next, the enclosures were surrounded by deep moats. *Carnivores, I presume*, she mused. The sign labeled the den as Wolverine. *Not one I would expect in a zoo.*

She stood on tiptoe, leaning over the railing searching the bushes for the wolverine perhaps lounging in the shade.

Ahem.

Sherry stood still. All the mornings birding with her mother kicked in and she searched for the source without moving. Dark black eyes peered at her from a branch four feet off the ground and much closer than Sherry expected.

Have you quite satisfied your voyeuristic appetite? A voice growled low in her mind.

For a moment, Sherry wondered if it were Madam swathed in black and brown fur. Honey being the better approach, she curtsied to the large female.

My apologies. I merely wished to satisfy my curiosity regarding the sign's accuracy. It is not common for a wolverine to be confined in a zoo.

My dear, quite true. If you ever see one, I hope you will let me know.

11

The wolverine stretched out her paws, the long white claws scratching on the branch. She laid her head down and shut her eyes.

"If you are done with your conversation, I'll show you to the office."

Sherry bit her tongue trying not to flinch as once again Micah spoke from just behind her shoulder. "I do wish you'd make a little more noise. It isn't polite to slip up on your guest."

"Madam Miriam said you're the new director. Then you aren't a guest."

"Director? Of what?"

"The zoo … using the muggle term. Harry Potter, forgive me. We'd rather think you are concierge of our home." Micah smile showing large and very sharp incisors. Before Sherry could question his statement, he continued, "This way. Madam Miriam's waiting for you in the Director's office." He offered Sherry his arm and stepped off in the direction he pointed.

"Micah." Sherry addressed the lad deciding honey was still the better approach. "What are you?"

"Me?" He smiled at her, the twinkle in his eye warning her another game began. "If you're as good as Miasma says you are, you'll figure it out."

"That is quite enough. I am honored by Miasma's assessment even though we just met, but if you are going to work for me, you will give me the respect to answer a direct question." She stamped her foot.

"I don't work for you."

She raised an eyebrow at him.

"I live here."

"You do?" She pursed her lips, feeling the answer just beyond her reach. The word 'home' reverberated in her mind.

"Yes, with my family. My father is unwell and we came here from the circus." Micah darted ahead and opened the door to a small building. She noticed the peeling paint and mildew odor … and something else she couldn't quite identify. The contrast between the first-rate animal enclosures compared to the rundown office intrigued her.

"Micah, what do you do here?"

He puffed out his chest. "I garden and feed the zoo animals." He escorted her farther into the gloomy interior. "My mother cooks for the rest."

"The ones who are hurt?"

"See, you're catching on!" He pivoted on his heel and pulled open the last door.

Light from a large picture window spilled into the hallway, driving away the darkness. Upon entering the small office, she nodded to Madam who sat behind an old wooden desk. Skirting around her, Sherry walked to the window. The river wound its way through the valley, the zoo walkways descending the hillside to meet at a boat dock. Brilliant flowers laced through the greenery. White marble benches dotted the lawn.

"Breathtaking!" Her eyes followed the movement, the multicolored birds fluttering with life.

"The only public entrance to the zoo is by ferry." Madam spoke, her tone gentle.

"And this is mine?" Sherry turned to face Madam, not wanting to tear her eyes away from the vista. "I mean, this is what you want me to do. Direct the zoo? It's not Whipsnade, but I'd say it could be much lovelier."

"Oh, my dear. Whipsnade it is not." Madam chuckled. "Dr. Ramhill, I speak for the Board when I offer the position as Director and Chief Veterinarian for the Waterton Zoo. The one and only veterinarian but it doesn't seem worth the expense to change the sign on the door."

Sherry grimaced at her.

"However, there is still one small matter we must resolve." Madam motioned for Micah to stand by her. "Your introductory letters make it quite clear you are an excellent veterinarian, and I would read between the lines to add healer. But do you have the talent to identify your patients correctly?"

Sherry opened her mouth to defend her extensive knowledge base once again, but Madam held up her hand.

"I do not mean what you recall from your class work. Are you able to identify this young man's species?" Madam took Micah's hand.

Her heart in her throat, Sherry chewed on the last statement and the question. *Identify him?* Her brow furrowed and she studied him through slitted eyes.

> *You're thinking too hard ... and loudly again.*
> Miasma rubbed against her leg. *Use your other eyes.*

Sherry rubbed her forehead, a headache striking her temple.

> *I'm not allowed to. My father was very clear. It angered him ... it is my Mother's way. Everything about her way angered him. After she died, we were forbidden to use any magick.*

She desperately wanted water ... with some scotch in it.

Micah scratched behind his ear, his fingers preternaturally long.

Pointed ears ... hair tufts. Sherry ran her eyes over his frame ending with the shadow curled behind him ... a long hairless tail. "Wererat. You are a wererat!"

Madam exhaled. "Very good." She pulled the visitor's chair closer to her and patted the seat.

"My Da prefers *Rattus intelligencious* so dubbed by Sir Nigel."

"My great uncle? You know him?"

"He's friends with my Da. He's almost a god in my nest. They traveled together in the circus."

"Oh, I am most certain my uncle was never in a circus." Sherry wrinkled her nose imagining Uncle Nigel in a red nose.

"Then you'd be mistaken for the second time today. He even tried his hand at Léger de Main for a while." Micah shook his head. "Da says he wasn't very good at it. Couldn't stop laughing at his own mistakes."

"Micah, will you please fetch your Mother's excellent tea?" Madam interrupted. Micah bowed and scurried from the office.

Sherry laughed at herself. *Why didn't I see it before?*

"Because you have been seriously hampered by your father's actions." Madam rifled through the papers on the desk. "And before I could trust you with the lives here, I needed to know you could overcome his programming. You exceeded my expectations."

Sherry sank into the chair. "I did, didn't I?"

"Yes, my dear. Now to the real business."

Chapter Two
Professor Lizzard and Sir Nigel speak

"Vincent? Is it you, old boy?"

Vincent Lizzard smiled, recognizing his old friend's exuberant voice. He held the receiver six inches from his ear. "Nigel, how wonderful you called. Have you recovered from the last … err … explosive incident in your laboratory?"

"By gosh, yes. Was quite an illuminating experience, old bean." Nigel guffawed. "But, at my wife's insistence, I've developed an interesting potion to limit the damage by future blowups."

Vincent cringed awaiting the anticipated pun.

"It's called Smithereen. Keeps bricks and glassware intact but allows chemical reactions to proceed. We shall have a fine time with it." His horsey laugh rolled from the phone.

"That is a wonderful development, Nigel." Vincent said. "Tell me, have you had a chance to analyze those samples I sent? There's been an increase in the flooding. I'm anxious to hear your findings." Vincent stood up and stretched his long, lean frame. He stepped to the laboratory window observing the garden below. He smiled as two black squirrels chased each other in race-around-the-tree tag.

"Tell me, Vincent, have your river rats found a new pathway to the demonic depths? The filtrate contained *Teppich* fibers … But the odd finding … the hair shows significant infernal elements … sulfur to be specific. But surely, I'm not saying anything new to you, my dear friend."

16

There was a worried pause. "I've jumped off on a different path, haven't I?"

Vincent could visualize his friend pushing his glasses up his nose, taking them off to polish them, and then placing both glasses and handkerchief back in his front jacket pocket. He smiled to himself. "They're in your pocket, Nigel."

"Good Lord, how on earth do you *do* that, Lizzard? Do you agree with my results?"

"Sadly, Nigel, I do. I'm not sure this bodes well for Miriam and her problems at the zoo. Samples twelve and thirteen derived from there." Silence on the line confirmed his worst fears.

Nigel chimed back in. "I wouldn't worry. You've got a young Ramhill on the job now. I'm quite certain Sherry can help you straighten things out. She's quite brilliant, you know. I'd say she takes after her old Uncle, but you'd call me a braggart."

"Nigel, what on earth are you talking about?"

"My niece. She has gone to work with Miriam. Haven't you met her yet?"

Vincent's heart fell deep in his chest. "No, Nigel. I haven't. Miriam does not find my company pleasant, so I have not been to the house in some time."

"I don't understand. We both know she adores you. She *cannot* be that daft. She's a *Wisdom* for Heaven's sake. Surely, she must understand how a curse works? I never would have agreed with Agatha to send Sherry so far away if I thought Miriam was still being so ... so adamant."

"She doesn't know—and can't be told—she's been cursed. You know it, Nigel. She has to figure this out for herself." Vincent sighed then straightened his back. "It's almost funny. Who'd ever think she'd have such a severe

17

reaction toward large green lizards? She champions all empowered creatures."

"You're a far kinder philosopher than I, my dear friend. I think she is quite dense frankly. I know … I know, curses and the ilk, but egad, Vincent!"

Vincent remained silent.

After a moment, Nigel continued. "I will put away my pout, as I am quite certain you are well aware an injustice has been served you both. I am just quite saddened, dear boy." Nigel cleared his throat. "On to the task at hand."

Vincent relaxed as Nigel outlined his plans to review and analyze the samples further. Nigel made no more comment concerning the troubles with Madam Miriam, and he was quite relieved. He enjoyed the friendship with the odd Englishman, but boundaries had to be observed until this curse could be released. If Nigel decided to interfere, Miriam could be badly harmed and it would not do. Not at all.

"So, you will arrange for more samples? I'll work up the schedule I'd like and transmit it by email if I can get the confounded system to work. All right then. Cheerio."

***

"Janitorial duties! Executive Assistant to the Mayor, my ass." Jonas grumbled "I can just imagine the rotational pull caused by my father spinning in his grave over my huge accomplishments." Tap. Tap. Tap. The sound echoed in the still morning.

"What the devil's that noise?" He rubbed his eye ridge. "Maybe someone's gotten ambition and are putting up some pictures. Not likely." Pausing in mid-sweep, he listened for Yancy's motorcycle engine. It paid to know when the Mayor would arrive before he actually did.

Tap. Tap. Tap. The door to the outer office flew open. Heels clicking on the wooden floor alerted him to the approaching figure. Brunette hair worked in an intricate chignon framed a heart-shaped face and deep green eyes. Jonas straightened to his full height as the curvaceous woman stopped in front of him.

"Would you please tell me exactly when someone in this administration deigns to arrive for work?"

Citrus. Sea Fennel. What a lovely scent. The irritation in her voice shocked Jonas from his musings. "I apologize, miss. Usually, I am seated behind this desk. But, you see, I like to have the office looking better in case we have someone important show up. I mean … uh … someone like you. I … um … I mean … um."

He wiped his face, a strained smile emerging from behind his hand. "Welcome to the Mayor's office. I am Jonas Bernstein, the Mayor's executive assistant. Won't you have a seat?"

"No, thank you. The chair seems to have a dustbin on it." Sherry stepped away from the proffered chair. She held her handkerchief to her nose.

"I will fix it in a New York minute. Please …" Jonas scrambled toward the chair, tripped on the rug and knocked the bin off. A dust storm billowed up aiming at her navy-blue suit.

She danced two steps farther away. "Really! If *this* is how things are handled here, I can understand completely how you'd allow so much pollution into the beautiful zoo"

The low tones in her voice sounded to Jonas like Miasma's warning before she struck. He shook his head to clear the imagined feline eyes under Sherry's golden lashes.

"Please, miss. Here, take my seat." He pulled his rolling chair out and wheeled it directly behind her. "Won't you please make yourself comfortable?"

19

Sherry inspected the chair then perched on the tattered tweed cushion.

Backing away, his elbow caught his water glass. As he fought to right it, it tipped forward sending a wave across the desk toward her lap. She sprang up, sending the chair against the wall. "You, sir, are a menace."

Jonas sopped up the water with the report he had spent the night completing. He took a deep breath and let out a belabored sigh.

Sherry let out a sigh in response then placed her hand on his arm. "Why don't we take it again from the top?"

Jonas knew his look of gratitude was fit for a puppy. He grimaced when she worked her mouth clearly trying to contain her laughter. He pulled the chair up and offered it to her again. She once again perched on the edge.

"Miss, may I ask your name?" Jonas put on his best Executive Assistant to the Mayor face. He pulled the other chair beside the desk and sat.

"Sherry Ramhill. I am the new veterinarian responsible for the Waterton Zoo." Sherry responded. "Madam Demarco is my sponsor."

"I know her quite well. She's my godmother." Jonas replied.

"I have spent the last week surveying the zoo. There are several enclosures damaged by the overflow during the heavy rains and the mildew is appalling. I have also been made aware the zoo is very important to several constituencies here."

"The zoo is also important to me, too." Jonas nodded. "The Mayor is deeply interested in the problem. We need to have a competent veterinarian in charge. I'm told you have great concern and passion for your patients." Jonas voice was low, soothing. He gazed at his notebook and sketched her face. *Strong jawline. Thick lashes.*

"When, sir? When do you expect the mayor to arrive?" Sherry tapped her fingernails on the desk.

"Truly, I don't know." Disappointment flash across her face. "You see, he believes in MBWA … that is, Management by Walking Around. He tours several parts of the city every day."

"I would wager he has not been to the Zoo lately or he would have done something about the deplorable conditions." Sherry pursed her lips.

Jonas fidgeted with his pencil. He took a breath. "I do have a suggestion. Have you spoken to Professor Lizzard at the Observatory? He'll be far more help than this office at the moment. He's quite a marvel scientifically and a darn good friend to the zoo, for sure. Let me give you a map and his number … though he usually doesn't answer. It's just as well to drop in on him. He likes cookies. Especially Madam DeMarco's cookies, but you might be a dab hand at them, too. No?"

Sherry shook her head but produced a small smile. "I am certain there is a bakery somewhere in town."

She rose.

Jonas stood, tipping his chair over in his haste.

"I will be back. Rest assured. And your mayor best have some answers. Good luck with your sweeping."

Chapter Three

Sherry Visits Professor Lizzard

Sherry rapped on the heavy metal door. She glimpsed motion through the side window. Peeking around the edge, she saw a shadowy figure moonwalking toward the door, a rolled-up paper in his hand.

"That pesky woodpecker. I'd best scare it away again or I won't have any peace." The door opened and Professor Lizzard swung the cylinder through the air, smacking the door frame well over Sherry's head. She stepped back from his paper bat.

Vincent stared down at her. "Yes?"

"Professor Lizzard? I am Sherry Ramhill. I hope you will forgive my rudeness in arriving unannounced." She pointed at his bat.

He lowered his hand to his side. "Woodpecker."

Sherry smiled her best and charged on. "Jonas … at the Mayor's office … suggested I should see you. I have brought cookies … and a dilemma. Do you have a moment or would you prefer to schedule a more convenient time?"

"So, this is what Nigel's eyes look like without his thick glasses!" He leaned down and studied her face. "Hmm. Never thought he'd translate into such a pretty woman."

Sherry fidgeted with the box, not certain how to reply to his scrutiny or the comment. "If I am inconveniencing you, I will go."

"Yes, yes. I mean, no, certainly not. Please come in." He stepped back. She crossed the threshold then sidestepped what appeared to be a long, scaled tail draped along the floor.

Am I crazy or am I really using different sight? She studied him in her peripheral vision. He remained tall and skeletally thin with thick white hair, but his skin had a definite green tint.

"I smell ginger. Who's been spilling the beans about my preferences? Madam Miriam, I assume." He bent closer to inspect the box she held.

"It was Jonas, sir."

Professor Lizzard's nictitating membrane closed and his shoulders drooped. He coughed, his hand to his mouth. He waved her into the cool interior.

Sherry looked about for a clear place to set the cookies. Books and papers littered the worktables and chairs, many open with brightly glowing rocks holding the pages. Shrugging, she hoisted her briefcase, balancing it on a pile of books stacked on the floor, hoping they were somewhat level. She set the cookies on top of the precarious tower which reached her midsection.

Gathering up the disheveled papers from the oak library chair, Lizzard gestured, with a bow, to the chair beside the cookie-laden tower. Two appeared in his hand on the back swing. He perched on the desk, leaning back to pull out a thermos from the file drawer. His tail counterbalanced him. He poured two mugs, holding one out to her.

She took the mug, noting the long, slightly spatulate fingers, his movements graceful.

"Australia."

"Excuse me?" She craned to look up him then shifted her chair slightly back to save her neck.

"Based on your first evaluation with your peripheral vision, your second evaluation should answer from where I hail. Australia is where I was … born." He smiled, showing small, even teeth. "Please, begin your story while I savor your delightful gift."

Sherry shifted her feet between the piles while gathering her thoughts. A mouse squeaked displeasure, standing tall on back paws, then scurrying under the desk, a cookie in her jaws. She silently tut-tutted his housekeeping.

"I wish to introduce myself as the new zoo director."

"I'm most certain you will be successful, my dear. Your uncle gave a glowing recommendation."

"Oh, my Uncle Nigel? I didn't know you were friends."

"Yes, friends and colleagues. Really, brothers-in-arms. But this is your story. Continue."

"I have inspected the zoo property and met some residents. I believe there are others who are still reticent. I understand their caution. I will proceed with due consideration." She shifted her feet again waiting for another rebuff from the little grey *mus musculus*. When none came, she continued. "I am delighted with the opportunity to work with such a wonderful community. But there are some concerns."

She lifted the cookie box and attempted to open her briefcase. The books wobbled alarmingly. She jumped as his cold fingers touched hers, removing the empty cookie box. *And the last cookie,* she noted. *I brought a dozen.*

His long tongue cleaned crumbs from his lips.

Smiling, she pulled a yellow pad from the briefcase. "Now, the current budget is inadequate for the necessary restocking of the infirmary. Not due to disregard by the previous director, I am sure." She hurried on. "But there are a few ailments I feel, in my professional judgment, need more aggressive and somewhat non-traditional treatments … which are expensive."

"Your professional judgment is what we depend upon." He nodded.

"Additionally, I am concerned with the water quality as well as the seepage filling several places in the zoo … including the office. There is a mold and mildew infestation. I am concerned for the food containment as well." She paused, looking through her notes while she gathered her courage.

"Professor, I assume you and Uncle Nigel know about the … uh … magical community. Since you are on the Board and I do see more about you than most, may I speak freely without you calling the gentlemen from the funny farm? It's been a shock to my system learning perhaps Stonehenge isn't Magick's single source in the universe. Madam DeMarco was quite delighted to demonstrate, though I may have the educational concepts, I am not nearly the expert my University assured me I had become."

"We wouldn't have hired you, Dr. Ramhill, if we weren't convinced you could do the work required." Lizzard's long fingers settled on her hand. "Madam Miriam has an … interesting perception regarding many things but she is quite wise. Quite wise indeed." His face saddened.

"I do not presume to know anything about the water system here but it seems as antiquated as the one in London. Especially the noxious mess Micah showed me yesterday." She wrinkled her nose. "Fortunately, Madam Miriam had Wellingtons which fit. The previous director must have been a large man."

"He was … initially." Professor Lizzard averted his eyes, shaking the box and scooping up the crumbs.

"Was? Was what? A man or a large man?" Sherry raised an eyebrow in concern.

"Yes, my dear, both."

"Professor Lizzard," Sherry squinted her eyes as she shifted to prosecutor mode. "What exactly happened to the previous director?"

"He … hem … he contracted a peculiar wasting disease. Didn't last very long, poor chap. The local physicians were stumped." Lizzard tapped the box again.

"And Madam Miriam?" Sherry pursued the point.

"Madam is astute in her healing arts. She determined it was brimstone toxicity." Lizzard busied himself pouring more tea, wincing as he brought the tepid brew to his lips. "Fresh tea, I think will be just the trick." He rose, towering over Sherry. "Do you wish more?"

"No, thank you," Sherry reached into her briefcase. "I can't say I am in agreement with the conclusion since brimstone is restricted to the inferno's third layer and I doubt Dr. … er … Dr. …"

"Alighieri." Lizzard filled in the gap.

"Now you are kidding me, Professor." Sherry rose, teetering between offense and amusement.

"Not at all, my dear." Lizzard strode to a back alcove, the undercounter LED lights coming on at his approach. A small Pullman kitchen fit into the corner. The stainless-steel countertops gleamed in the intense light.

"Hailed from Florence. Educated at Universidad de León. Highly qualified." Lizzard stared at his electric kettle. "Considered himself quite a poet."

"Professor Lizzard, the situation is serious and I do not feel we are getting to the point." Sherry tapped her foot.

"Now, my dear, please don't take offense. Have a seat and I'll bring the tea." Lizzard poured the steaming water over fresh tea leaves. "Let's start again. You have something to show me, I am certain. Given the papers in your hands."

Sherry looked at the sheath she held. She huffed, then unfolded a large map. "As I was saying, I do not presume to know anything about the sewer system, but given the topography in this surrounding area, I would say something is retarding the proper drainage. Would you be so kind as to point out the waste treatment plant for the city?"

Lizzard bent over with his nose so close to the map, Sherry wondered if he needed glasses. He drew a finger along the river. "The town center is here and the zoo is there." He jabbed a fingernail at a spot where the river turned at a thirty-degree angle. "The plant is about here. The pump station is here." He straightened, rubbed his back for a moment. "The city council was embarking on a storm water management program … young Jonas' brainchild. The storm water system is antiquated though not as old as London, I promise you. The last few years the rains have been heavier than normal, increasing the problem."

"From what I read on Jonas' desk, there is a company proposing to solve the problem for the city in return for a building permit. It looked like a large project from the thick dossier."

Lizzard raised a scaly eyebrow at her.

"I read upside down." Her face warmed, abashed. "I wasn't deliberately prying. It is just an old habit."

"Sounds like it comes in handy." Lizzard handed her a fresh mug, eyeing the empty box. "Dr. Ramhill. Sherry, if I may?"

She nodded.

"Sherry." He started again. "First off, I like you." Pink rose on his cheeks. "I don't say it often … or to many people. But you have spunk and I respect that." He picked up his own mug and finished it in one go. "Second, your information is beginning to pull some interesting observations into a disturbing picture."

He squatted onto a foot stool, looking Sherry eye to eye. She sat forward on the chair's edge. "I obtained soil samples from the drainage areas. The analysis shows a temporal shift indicating some interaction between the planes."

She blinked as she processed the statement.

"Do you know what that means?" Lizzard stared at her.

Sherry opened her mouth then closed it. "No, Professor, I really do not. I was lousy at physics, and mentioning the planes sent me into a fog."

Lizzard rocked back on his stool. "I see." His eyelids, both in each eye, closed for a moment. "It means somewhere here we have or had a visitor from somewhere else and he or she is leaving a chemical footprint. If your Uncle and I can determine the identity and approximate elemental mixture, we may be able to deduce the origin and, therefore, most probably, the identity."

"Do you think it is hostile?"

"I'd prefer to think not." He gathered up the mugs, set them on the counter and paced back to Sherry. She craned her neck to look up at his full height. He stabbed his finger at three points on the map, circumnavigating the zoo grounds. "We need soil samples from these locations. Eight to ten inches deep will do." He pulled open the desk drawer and rummaged in the back. He held out three large mouthed specimen jars. "About a cup will be fine. But no leaves or grass."

28

Sherry nodded and tucked the jars into her bag. She stood and offered her hand. "It has been a pleasure, sir."

"Oh, no, the pleasure was all mine." Vincent eyed the empty cookie box while clasping her hand in a chilly handshake. "No matter how fleeting."

He held the door for her then stepped out onto the catwalk encircling the observatory base. "You can see the zoological park from here." He pointed across the river.

"It is lovely," Sherry surveyed the grounds. "I have walked those paths over the past few days, but I did not realize how beautiful they are … entwined vines leading to the gardens at the top." She leaned over the railing. "And you can see Madam DeMarco's house as well. There she is on the widow's walk."

Vincent stepped forward. He stared at the slight figure.

Sherry straightened her spine and stuck out her chin. "I will get you the samples you need. I promise you I will."

Vincent laughed, stepping back from the rail. "I'm certain of it. Put a Ramhill on the case and it is as good as solved."

They shook hands once again. Sherry stared at her fingers coming away with warmth now the Professor was outside in the sunlight.

"By the way," Lizzard called to her as she walked to her car. "Sir Nigel wished to know if you have made any friends."

Sherry gritted her teeth, biting back a snide reply. "I hope I just have." She slipped into the SUV and fired it to life. Backing carefully along the cliff edge, she turned the vehicle down the hill.

Chapter Four

Sherry explores the Waterline Bar and identifies the problem

Sherry shimmered down the stairs into the below street-level barroom, a star in the darkness. Her gold high heels tapped on the stone steps. The violet silk threads in her tweed suit jacket reflected all the light the gloom would relinquish.

She paused at the bottom, allowing her eyes to adjust. The burly men, hunched over their stew and beer, raised their fingers to their foreheads, tipping imaginary hats. She smiled at them, feeling the appreciative stares as she approached the bar.

Perched on a bar stool, her high heels dangled. The bartender wiped the stone counter and waited, no expression on his pale face.

"My goodness." She ran a nail tip along the smooth surface. "It is sufficiently gloomy to be two in the morning. Not quite time for despair, but running close, and yet ..." She looked back at the door she'd entered. "It was quite sunny and bright a moment ago." She leaned toward the bartender. "What's your secret?"

Gino shrugged, his long dark hair brushing his shoulders. He swiped at an imaginary stain, his long fingernails scraping the surface.

Sherry twisted in her seat looking around the room. She noted the tables with varied faces, few women among the

30

customers but the ones present equally as large as their male companions. Most stared at their plates, only one or two looking up to meet her eye.

"I feel quite at home here." She studied the bottles lined up behind the bar, the shelves surrounding an open space usually sporting a mirror, its absence she found interesting.

"May I have a double MacCallan neat?"

Gino reached for the bottle. Sherry slipped from the stool and, walking past the open seats, chose one directly next to the silent man seated at the far end. She studied his dark wavy hair, the lock falling over his forehead as he bent forward writing in the large ledger. She imagined him in black rather than the grey turtleneck and khaki pants he wore.

Nick glanced up, his scowl indicating displeasure at the interruption. Sherry assessed him as carefully as the Royal Navy supreme commander. Long lashes veiled her thoughts. He glanced at his bartender.

Gino recapped the bottle. "Boss, heads up." He slid the lowball along the bar. A giggling pixy flashed up from the shadows, preceding the glass with a cocktail stir, sweeping in best curling style. Without taking his eyes from his boss, Gino grabbed a tall glass and trapped the pixy cutting off the high-pitched noise. Gino shook his finger at the fluttering creature, its nose against the glass.

Nick caught the lowball before it careened onto the paperwork.

"And how large a glass do you have in mind for me if I irritate you?" She murmured as Nick set the lowball within her reach.

He stared her.

Okay, Sherry thought, *this may be a long chess match.* She smoothed her jacket. *Bring it on.*

"I suspect it would take something more like leather handcuffs and silk ropes." He nodded at the staring workmen. "And a stronger man than I to get past your admirers."

Sherry flashed a bright smile at the crowd. The motion released them, conversation starting again and mugs raised. She turned back to Nick, her hands surrounding her drink. "How *energizing*."

"We don't get many day folk in here." Nick looked down at the ledger adding another note.

"Day folk? But all these people are here." She swept her hand at the full tables.

"They're the Midnight Crew." He didn't lift his eyes from the page.

"Midnight crew?" Sherry waited for his response.

"On the docks overnight."

"Isn't that work dangerous?" Sherry willed him to look up, wanting to look into his dark eyes again.

Nick took a breath as if to answer.

Loud footfalls echoed from the far corner. A door, hidden in shadows, swung open revealing dimly lit stairs. A tall man in a once-white jacket appeared, a grey shag carpet draped over his shoulder. The stained roll lurched in his grasp spraying muddy water across the room.

"Christian!" A large gargoyle stood from the table, overturning his chair.

"Sorry, Arnie. Can't stop it from shaking. Sopping wet." Christian tossed his own long loose blond hair, sending more water in Arnie's direction.

Arnie growled, wiping his basketball-sized face with the small napkin.

Christian stalked straight through the tables, passing close by the stools lining the bar.

Nick grabbed Sherry under the arms and lifted her over the bar into Gino's arms, just as the creature's maw opened, emitting a sonorous belch. The tubular head thrashed, circular rows of teeth mouthed the stools, sending them clattering to the floor. Inch long fangs scraped along the stone bar, the screech shattering the glass, setting the pixy free. Hands on his ears, he dove under the bar.

Christian bent his knees, hefting the squirming mass higher on his shoulder. In the process, the mouth gobbled up Sherry's purse.

"I could use a little help here!" Christian nodded at Sherry now standing behind the bar. "Pretty woman! New help? More appealing than pale boy there." He carted the rumbling, struggling mess into the narrow hallway, the purse strap trailing along the floor.

"Not on my bed! Please!" High pitched giggles issued from under the bar. Gino slammed wine glasses down on the shelf. The high-pitched screams shattered two, spraying glass across the floor. Gino switched to beer mugs, capturing the pixies. He vaulted over the bar and disappeared down the hall behind Christian.

Nick stood and took a step after him before a hand fell on his arm.

"Cod liver oil." Sherry sipped on the scotch, dabbing her perfect British Red lips with a napkin. "And you owe me a new pocketbook."

"I beg your pardon?" Nick stopped in midstride.

"It is a *Verlottert teppich*. They do not usually go so … hiccuppy. It must be eating the wrong things. Cod liver oil will do the trick." She looked at Nick. "If you must, corn oil

"Are you well coordinated? I have a brother who looks it, but who's always tripping over some imaginary item or another."

Nick stepped over the broken crates without glancing back at her. Glass and spilled liquor coated the floor. He slipped, nearly falling as the *teppich* wrenched free from Gino. Teeth sunk into the edge of a large wooden box, tearing a gaping hole in the corner. Dirt poured out.

Gino moaned, grabbed up an empty bucket and shoved it under the cascade. Christian tackled the creature, straddling it, bull riding it back to the floor. Bloody gashes showed through his tattered sleeves.

"Watch out for the quills." He gasped, fighting for breath.

Sherry leaned over Nick's shoulder. "They don't mind bottles. Just shove the whole thing in. It's going to split soon and then we'll have tiny—very hungry—teeth everywhere. GO!"

Nick set two bottles behind him. Holding the other, he squatted at the head end, timing the bucking. He shoved the first bottle into the shark-like maw. He waved his empty hand behind his back, waiting for the next bottle. Sherry set the bottle in his hand. He swung forward depositing the second between snaps. He reached back for the third, but his hand remained empty. He glanced back at Sherry as she leaned over his shoulder.

"I think two will be sufficient. This is a young one. You can tell by the teeth."

Nick sat backwards as the *teppich* issued a gullet-cracking yawn. Brown eyes with long, luxurious lashes emerged from under the grimy fur. They blinked at him, once, twice, the lids closing.

"And if you give it a little scritch right there," Sherry pointed at the inert mass. "Where you'd imagine a shoulder might be, you might be rewarded with a giggle or two."

Christian reached around from his position atop the creature and ran his fingers along the spot she indicated. A high-pitched giggle filled the room. Sherry placed her hand on Nick's shoulder and leaned over him. He stiffened at the contact.

"Don't move," she commanded. Another yawn opened the mouth. "I wish to retrieve my pocketbook." She poured the third bottle into the gullet. It swallowed and yawned again. Sherry pointed into the mouth. "There it is! You can just about reach the strap!" She overbalanced.

Nick caught her around the hips, her weight on his shoulder. Sherry waved her arms, attempting to back pedal and regain her balance. A backwards shove from Nick landed her squarely on her feet. She pulled down her jacket, brushing her skirt.

"I really don't want to lean into those teeth. Do be a dear and retrieve it for me." She tapped Nick on the shoulder. He waited for the next yawn. The maw opened, jaw bones cracking. Nick snatched the trailing strap, pulling the purse loose, the momentum launching the purse over his shoulder and into the hallway.

"Good thing I don't carry any breakables. How rude." She stomped into the hall, picking up the purse by the strap using only two fingers. "Well, this one is ready for the trash bin."

She returned to the storeroom door in time to see Christian motioning Nick back down to the floor.

Hmm, Sherry thought. *I suppose I could have sounded more grateful.* She looked directly at Christian still astride the *teppich.* "Do not move yet. *Teppichs* become grumpy if awakened too soon. We must wait until it snores."

Christian nodded, lighting the room with a brilliant smile. She felt a warmth flow through her chest, contrasting with the cold shoulder she leaned over. Rattling drew her attention. Gino swept the remaining dirt into the bucket.

"Gino, be a dear and fetch them some towels, will you? Then Arnie is awaiting his reward."

Gino backed out into the hallway, the bucket clutched in his arms. The three waited without a word until a loud snore emanated from the *teppich*.

Sherry nodded to Christian. He stood, his movements slow and stepped clear. Another snore rewarded his stealth.

"They are not indigenous to this area. Do you have a shop which specializes in the exotic? I happen to think they are lovely, but sadly, few agree."

Nick did not look around nor respond to her question.

Gino handed a towel to Christian and tossed one over Nick's shoulder. Christian rubbed down his arms and dried his hands.

"Introductions are in order." He half bowed without dropping eye contact with Sherry. "I am Christian McMillan … lately from Scotland. And you are?"

She gulped, swept up in his ice blue eyes. "Sherry." She found her voice, the firmness increasing once the first sounds passed her lips. "Doctor Sherry Ramhill. I am the new zoo director." Her eyes traveled over his muscled physique. He chuckled. She turned away quickly, breathing deeply to beat off her blush. "Ahem …" she cleared her throat and looked at Nick. "We did not have a proper introduction, either."

He turned to her from his position on the floor and held out his wine-covered hand. She stared at the deep red stains on his khaki pants. "Nick Szabo." He got his feet under him and rose to tower over her. "I own this place." He rubbed his hands on his pants. "And I'd best change. Excuse me." He stepped over the snoring *teppich*. "How long will it sleep?"

"I'd say about six hours. Until I know what it has been eating, I cannot say with certainty." She reached for Christian's sleeve and surveyed the gashes. "I don't see any needing stitches, but a methacrylate smear would be in order."

Nick harrumphed and disappeared into his office.

"May I buy you a drink?" Christian removed her hand from his arm and indicated she should proceed him back into the bar. "Or should I change from these muddy clothes, first?"

"A little mud never bothers me, and we have earned a drink on the house." She reached for the barstool, but Christian steered her by the elbow to a secluded booth. She smiled at him and slid onto the bench. He settled beside her. Gino arrived with a dark stout sporting a large head and two lowball glasses containing MacCallan Scotch.

"Oh, you are darling, but I cannot possibly drink them both."

"For the boss." Gino set the glasses down with a sharp snap.

"Oh." Sherry looked at her hands then took a deep breath. When she raised her face, she smiled at Christian. "I do get ahead sometimes."

Christian laughed then took a long drink. She marveled how he avoided the inevitable foam mustache. "We all do at times."

She felt better immediately. Christian left the seat to return with pretzels. He ate several in quick succession. "Didna have time for lunch what with the … what did you call it?"

"*Teppich*." She looked at him. "*Verlottert teppich*, to be precise. A species identified in the Black Forest."

Christian laughed. "Scruffy carpet."

Sherry's eyes lit up.

"Must have been a scientist with a yen for comedy." Christian laughed again.

"My great uncle, Sir Nigel Ramhill." She continued, "He is an alchem—." She paused as Nick slid into the seat across from her, his knee knocking against hers.

"What did I miss?" Nick picked up the lowball and drained it.

"Oh," Sherry stared in dismay. *One should not disrespect excellent Scotch in such a boorish manner.* She started to correct him but reconsidered as she noticed he was now dressed in the anticipated black turtleneck and black jeans. *Much better*, she thought. A pleasant expression on her face, she filled him in. "We were discussing the *teppich* and wondering how it got here. They are native to Europe. I would never have dreamed one would find its way across the pond."

Nick stared at her.

She met his eyes. "But I have been informed lately I do not know much about this continent." The two men remained silent. "I am a quick study. Where did you find this one?"

Christian shifted his eyes to Nick. Sherry's skin prickled at the unspoken question between them. Nick nodded slightly and reached for the refill Gino slipped on the table.

Christian met Sherry's eye. "Stuck in the intake on a barge."

"Oh, the poor thing. It must have been very frightened."

"Not nearly as the mechanic trying to pull it out … when the mouth opened." Christian chuckled.

"This is highly unusual behavior. They frequent waterways mainly underground and rarely venture out where there are mechanical objects. Contact with metals distresses them and they are shy around people."

"This one was finishing the exhaust pipe, one bite at a time."

"This is not good." Sherry shook her head. "They eat metal when the population density drives them out from their preferred habitat. They are herbivores under normal circumstances. This means there are many. I wager they have something to do with the issue with the sewers."

Thunder rumbled, rattling the bottles behind the bar. Two small figures wrapped in newspapers tumbled down the stairs. Unwrapping from the sports page, the smaller helped his companion to emerge from the want ads. Sherry studied the two intently, her forehead furrowing.

"Sherry?" Christian broke her concentration.

"Sorry, just practicing." She looked at his puzzled expression. "I don't know why I feel so comfortable with you ...." She glanced at Nick. "Both. But I have never been good at secrets ... or making friends."

Christian patted her hand. "I find that hard to believe. You've won Arnie's heart at least." He nodded at the gargoyle who grinned. "What brings you to the Colonies?"

"My great aunt sent me to get away from an unpleasant situation. I was campaigning for equal rights for our different friends, and it was not viewed with favor. So, I was packed off to take over the zoo. There is so much I need to learn about this country. May I count on your help?"

Christian nodded. "Of course. But what were you practicing by staring at Marty?"

"Well, I have dealt with creatures such as the *teppich* ... studied extensively but I was not trained to detect shape shifters. See the gentleman there?" She leaned over the table, dropping her voice and drawing the two men close. "He may look like a little person but he's a wererat."

Nick and Christian laughed out loud, setting her back in her seat.

"Dr. Ramhill, please don't be offended. Certainly, he is. Marty and his family are valued friends." Nick smiled at her trying to use Christian's technique to set people at ease. His sharp canines gleamed in the dim light and Sherry drew farther back. Nick charged on. "What I mean to say is this bar is neutral territory where the other folks, the Midnight Crew, can relax and enjoy a drink. And Madrecita's cooking."

The magic words materialized Gino with a sizzling platter. The aroma of grilled meat and spicy sauce sent saliva streaming through Sherry's mouth. A slight figure behind him carried plates and a tortilla cozy.

"Micah?" Sherry stared at the young man.

"Dr. Ramhill. I didn't expect to see you here." Micah handed her a knife and fork.

"Do you work here?"

"Yes, ma'am. When my chores are done at the zoo." He gathered up the empty glasses and headed for the swinging kitchen door. "That's my Da at the bar with Uncle Ustes." He nodded his head at the small figure hoisting a tall amber ale. "He'll tell you the stories about Mr. Nigel if you ask nicely." He chuckled. "Or even if you don't." He danced between the tables picking up empty mugs as he went.

"Micah has many talents." Sherry watched him glide through the swinging door. "But isn't he too young to work in an establishment serving alcohol?"

Nick laughed. "How old do you think he is?"

Sherry opened her mouth then closed it without uttering a sound. "I'm doing it again, aren't I? Accepting things at face value without looking deeper." She glanced at Christian who nodded. "I won't even hazard a guess. It would amuse you too much." She stuck out her tongue at Nick then scooped the fajita mix onto a tortilla. He chuckled and followed suit. Christian reached for his second.

The street level door slammed open, wind swirling through the bar carrying napkins into the air. Two figures hurried through the door, their cloaks shedding water. Lightning illuminated the stairwell.

Sherry listed her objectives. "All right then, we need to find the nest and determine the population density." The thunder rolled through the room shaking dust from the ceiling. "My goodness, I need to get back to the zoo to check on the animals in the lower compounds. I am not dressed appropriately for an excursion into the wet." She nudged Christian. He slipped out to allow her to rise. She caught the look exchanged between the two men. "I will be back in an hour. Sooner if you let Micah accompany me." She raised a sculptured eyebrow at Nick. "And a brolly?"

"Umbrella." Christian jumped in to save Nick from asking.

Nick rose and spoke with Micah as he cleared the tables vacated by the denizens leaving by the underground door. Micah nodded toward his father, who slipped from the bar stool and waved at Gino. He approached the two.

"Marty, have you met Dr. Ramhill?" Nick placed a hand on Marty's shoulder.

"Haven't had the pleasure though the boy here tells a good tale about her first day." Marty slapped Micah on the back nearly overbalancing him. Glasses and mugs rattled on his tray.

43

"Would you mind guiding her through the underground to the zoo?"

"Not at all. Though Madrecita's masterpieces are making my mouth water, I'm expected at home for dinner with the brood." Thunder rattled the narrow basement windows. "I'd rather not go back out in that." He eyed the water pouring down the narrow glass.

Marty stuck out his hand. "Pleased to meet one of Nigel's relatives. Micah tells me you don't know much about the old man. Or at least about his early years."

Sherry shook Marty's hand firmly. "I am compiling a rather lengthy list regarding things I did not know. I hope you will enlighten me further." She leaned close to his ear. "Especially if there is something to embarrass him at the holidays."

Marty guffawed and slapped her on the back. She wobbled but did not shy away from the blow. "I like you, girl. Come along. Dinner waits for no man in my house."

Christian handed her a large black umbrella. "It will be dripping in the tunnels. Be careful."

Sherry noticed the sincerity in his eyes and smiled at him. "Thank you." She put a finger against his breastbone. "Now, do not leave without me." He nodded solemnly. *Like fun, you will not*, she thought.

"Sherry." Nick put a hand on her arm, his cold fingers chilling through her sleeve. "What do we do with the *teppich*? We can't leave it in the storeroom."

"No, of course not. Is there access to the storm drains from here?"

Nick nodded.

"Then I'd very carefully … not to awaken it … take it to the edge. When it wakes up, it will slip into the water. They are very adept at maneuvering in and out of the water." She looked to Christian. "You might wish to do it soon as it sleeps the deepest at first. And you do not want to get another set of clothes dirty."

He grimaced and nodded his understanding.

Marty led her through the dark hallway from which Christian had emerged. Four steps into the hall, the smooth wooden grain panel gave way to rough brick. Track lighting extended into the distance. Several feet into the corridor, Marty guided her to the left. The new passageway was lit intermittently with bare bulbs. Trying to avoid the steady dripping from the ceiling, Sherry tripped over the iron rail barely above the dirt surface. Marty caught her arm.

"Thank you." She marveled at the strength in the man whose face came just to her midsection.

"My pleasure, miss. I encouraged your uncle to lift weights with me but he disliked sweating."

Sherry laughed, the sound echoing in the tunnel. "That is the Uncle Nigel I know." She noticed a second rail parallel to the first. "Is this a subway? I didn't see any stations in town."

"Not a functioning one. Alfred E. Beach's folly. He was an inventor … came here at Madam Miriam's invitation. To bring progress to the city or so she convinced the town council."

A large object loomed in the dim tunnel. Two huge reflective eyes peered at them, unblinking. Marty did not slow, so Sherry trusted the eyes were not attached to hungry teeth. As they approached, the shadow resolved into a wooden subway car, the operator's compartment without glass and the passenger seats open without roof or sides. "This looks like an amusement park trolley." Sherry ran her fingers along the wooden rail surprised they came away clean.

"I keep it shined up … a hobby." Marty pointed to the large fan blades at the rear. "Pneumatic pressure powered it. Blew up quite a dust cloud from the histories I've read."

Sherry peered at a brass plate on the side. "But this says the car was built in 1868." She straightened and put her hands on her hips. "You said Madam Miriam brought the inventor here." She stared at him.

"She's a permanent fixture in this town and a gentleman never asks a lady her age." Marty stopped, putting his finger to his lips. Sherry froze. She listened intently, but all she could hear was the dripping water and its echo.

"Good." Marty started off at a galloping pace. "Can you keep up, Miss?"

Sherry lengthened her stride, regretting the high heels. She gritted her teeth and, ducking her head, caught up with him straining to stay even. "You said good. Is there something we are running from or to?"

"To, my dear. I hear my wife's lovely voice. Anastasia doesn't tolerate tardiness. She puts the food on the table hot and expects it to be eaten immediately." Marty turned right and disappeared into a narrow hallway. "And with my brood, it will be. Don't want to go hungry tonight!"

Sherry caught the corner, swung around and came nose to nose with him.

"Sorry, Miss. Should have warned you about the stairs. Careful, now. They're a bit steep." He held out his hand. She closed the umbrella, grateful again for his strength as the riser height was higher than normal.

"Now you are going to tell me Mr. Beach was a tall man."

"He and his crew all were. They forgot what it was like for the normal man. Some lineage with the giants, I'd say."

Sherry gulped. Giants were not in her textbooks, either. *But then again, would they be considered animals?* She wondered as her thighs burned.

Marty opened the outer door. Wet wind threatened to topple her back down the stairs.

He hauled her up the last step. She opened the umbrella, hanging on to it double-fisted. The wind whipped the umbrella away. Marty picked her up in his arms and galloped quickly across the compound to the administration building porch. Sherry clung to him, her face buried in his broad neck. He set her upright. Even under roof, the wind drove the rain sideways soaking them both. Marty hauled open the door. "Get inside," he ordered. Once she cleared the threshold, he shut the door firmly behind her and ran back across to the trolley access.

"Good grief." Sherry's words echoed in the empty waiting room. She pulled off her high heels and dripped her way to the director's office. *Thank goodness, I had the sense to bring work clothes to the office.* She stripped to underclothes and pulled on her khaki jumpsuit. *At least it isn't cold.* The cinder block walls ran with moisture from the humid air.

She rifled through the closet until she found the Wellingtons. Feeling scrutinized, she turned from the closet. Eight black eyes peered at her from a rattan basket mounted on the wall. She reached into the desk drawer and opened the oatmeal box. Sifting through it with her fingers, she pulled out the squirming mealworms. She held her hand out palm up.

Three heartbeats passed until the smallest sugar glider launched from the nest box and landed on her forearm. It grabbed up a meal worm and chomped contentedly. She deposited the remaining worms on the desktop. The glider jumped off, reaching for another treat as the other members of the nest glided to the desk scrambling over the meal. They finished the wiggling worms, then scurried up the pole lamp and launched for home.

Home, she thought. *Two weeks. This is beginning to feel like home. Now to find a torch.* She pulled out the long black flashlight and rummaged through the drawer for extra batteries. *Ah hah, this girl may have learned from a book, but I am getting smarter about this world.*

She jerked the filing cabinet drawer open. The shriek pierced her ears. *In this humidity, everything is going to rust, even the iron in my hemoglobin.* She chuckled at her own joke and ran her fingers along the file labels. Pulling a thick one out, she laid the contents on the desk. *Utility lines, compound moats ... come along, there has to be a sewer access.* She placed her finger on the symbol for the subway entrance. *A major drawback about the zoo is the limited access for the public ... only by water. The subway would make a tremendous difference.*

Forked lightning lit the window in the office, flashing two ... three ... four times in quick succession. The desk lamp flicked twice and went dark. She picked up the flashlight, thumbing the switch. *I really do have to check the lower compounds.* The telephone rang, startling her and she dropped the light on the desk. Thunder rolled up the valley rattling the windows. *Steady on.* She straightened her shoulders and lifted the receiver.

"Hello."

"Sherry, are you all right? The weather is frightful."

Sherry sighed at Madam's voice. "I've been to the Mayor's office who sent me to Professor Lizzard. Then I explored the funny bar in town. Due to the rain, Marty brought me along the trolley way back to the zoo. It has been quite an adventure." She heard Madam draw in breath. She forged ahead. "I regret I did not send word. I have to check the lower compounds. I am worried about the water level."

48

"My dear, you do not have to account for every moment. My concern is for your continued safety. I will send Arnie to fetch you."

She does sound concerned, not annoyed. "Arnie? Lovely. I will call when I have finished my circuit. Thank you. Goodbye." She hung up before Madam could respond.

Starting at the subway entrance, she traced her finger down along the zoo walkways until she came to the lowest point. Peering at the notations, she discovered the pumping station which circulated water in the pools and streams throughout the zoo. Beside the building was the symbol for sewer. She tied back her hair, gathered up the flashlight and prepared to conquer the weather.

Chapter Five

The Mayor considers an offer and visits the Waterline Bar

Yancy Fairhaven felt rumpled. He yawned and looked deep into his well-worn coffee mug. *This thing surely needs rinsing, if not full consideration by biohazard experts.* His wife would argue his cup now supported a small microbial city requiring his mayoral capabilities as well. He stretched, gazing down at his light brown corduroy pants, leather vest and crumpled white shirt. *Never should have given up the open road. Running a town! I should be riding with Triss hanging on behind me.*

He rubbed his face then rose to rinse his coffee cup. The water sputtered in the sink, resisting going down the drain.

"Mr. Mayor. May I remind you *again*, we have a water crisis? We have a meeting with the Santos Development Group in the morning. They're very interested in helping us, sir. Have you had a chance to review their proposal? We stand to gain a great deal from their generous offer."

Yancy grimaced at his fresh-faced aide. "Jonas, I've got to tell you, the idea worries me. What is it they expect to gain? It makes me uncomfortable. Our sewer problems have been around for a while. Why their sudden interest in this backwater town? It doesn't feel right to me."

Jonas looked up from his notes. "There is such a thing as good luck. By the way, Mr. Szabo called … wants you to stop by his bar. Said there is an interesting problem you might want to know about."

Yancy laughed. "Yeah. I'm always interested in finding out about more problems in the city, aren't I?" He sighed. He needed a drink, but it had nothing to do with coffee. *Cripes! Even my rumples are crumpled.* "Jonas, I'm gone. Maybe I can find a quiet table and review this damn contract."

"Sir, you really don't want to take the contract with you, do you?" His face paled. "You remember the last time you went to Mr. Szabo's bar? Your briefcase was ... er ... macerated. The term you used."

Yancy straightened his shoulders to work out the kinks. "Jonas. We need to find you a Hog. You worry too much."

"I keep Kosher ... most days."

Yancy laughed as he left the building. A crack of lightning hastened his steps. Just as he reached the outside access to the bar, the skies opened above him and drenching rain fell. He pulled his slouch hat lower and plunged into the dark stairwell.

It's puzzling how this tavern refuses to let anything but gloom and despair enter. The wind whipped the doorknob from his hand, slamming it back against the stone wall. Yancy wrestled it closed. He turned expecting staring eyes upon him.

The room was empty of patrons. Yancy stood still, waiting for his eyes to adjust. Gino looked up, his mop stopped in mid-swipe. He nodded toward the back booth. Tables and chairs littered the room, more disheveled than usual as if the patrons fled in a hurry. Water trailed across the room from the back entrance to the storeroom hallway. Gino swiped at it without much energy.

And an odd time to mop the floors, Yancy thought. He stepped gingerly through the mess to the back booth.

"Tough night already, Nick?" He peered at Nick hidden in the gloom. "I mean, it's barely 5 o'clock." He took off his hat, shook the rain onto the floor. He slid into the opposite bench.

Gino growled, swiping the mop over Yancy's brown leather boots. Yancy shoved his feet under the table.

Nick waved Gino away.

"Yes. It's been … busy." Sharp white teeth gleamed in the shadow.

Yancy stared at the vivid scratch across Nick's jaw. "I see. Well, perhaps now isn't a good time." He rose from the seat, stopped from leaving by Nick's hand on his arm.

"No, I regret my foul mood. It isn't aimed at you." He signaled for Gino to return. "Gino, please bring the Mayor his usual and ask Madricita for a plate."

Yancy eased back into the chair. On one hand, he trusted Nick. Primarily because he needed him as the liaison with his alternative constituency who, he admitted, had been instrumental in his win over the twenty-four-year incumbent in the last election. But on the other hand, close involvement with said constituency did make him uneasy at times, Nick being first on the list.

I didn't used to feel that way about him, he thought as he realized there was no warmth on his arm where Nick's hand rested. *But now.* He let the thought drop as Gino presented a dirty martini with extra dirt. It was a double.

***

Nick followed Yancy up the stairs. The mayor turned to the railing overlooking the river and studied the grey roiling waters flowing past the shore.

"Nick, thanks as always for keeping me updated. I'm not certain what to do with the story of rolls of shaggy carpeting clogging up the storm drains." He stared at the roiling water, imagining previously described teeth below the surface.

"Yancy, you're doing a good job for this town." Nick stepped up beside him.

His eyes still on the river, Yancy spoke, his voice barely heard above the rushing water. "Nick, I didn't expect a compliment from you."

Nick leaned his forearms on the iron railing, the wind filling his windbreaker. "We're not back in high school. It's not my job to torment the geeks anymore."

Yancy snorted. He punched Nick in the arm. "I remember you as a pretty good student."

Nick stepped away from the railing, rubbing his arm, a broad smile on his face. "Well, at least, you've learned how to deliver a decent punch."

"Boxing. In college." Yancy looked back at the water.

"You've been back in town for almost five years. After those years on the road, is wanderlust getting to you? It's got to be hard staying here. Especially with a Traveler wife."

"You know, Nick, I thought it would be. Don't get me wrong, I still have thoughts about climbing on the bike. Leaving everything here … but something makes it worthwhile. I don't know what when the town's folk are so resistant to change." He paused then looked Nick in the eye. "What do you know about Triss?"

Nick quirked an eyebrow. "Not much. I met Travelers in several different ports around the world. There's an aura about them. That's all."

Yancy thought about that answer for a moment. Shifting gears, he said, "But why are you still here? You got away right after high school, too."

"If ending up in the Navy is getting away, yeah, you'd be right."

Yancy turned his back to the wind, facing Nick. "You got to see the world ... a world I may never see."

"And you've seen more of this country than I probably will." Nick looked at him. "To be honest, I never intended to come back here. But when I got a medical discharge, the only place I could imagine was this grubby river town." He glanced back at the stairway down to the bar. "And the bar. After Mom died, I understood why Dad buried himself in it. But even before, his heart was always here and with the Midnight Crew"

"Medical discharge? I thought you opted out. You okay?"

Nick smiled. "Bradycardia. Unexplained."

"Brady what?" Yancy furrowed his brow.

"Heart beats too slowly. They were afraid I'd faint under stress."

"Do you?"

"No ... or at least I haven't yet." Nick chuckled.

Yancy turned back to watch the eddies in the water. "You know I don't talk about your ... patrons. But as I've gotten to know them, I see why he loved and supported them." Yancy ran his hand along the iron railing. "I'm well aware we have to be cautious with the mundanes but if they'd only give Madrecita or Marty a chance."

Nick laughed. "Not highly likely."

"I know. I probably wouldn't have either before I met Triss. She opened my eyes."

The two men stood in silence watching the flotsam and jetsam float by. Tree limbs tangled in the anchor chains of the river barges tied to the dock below. Wet wind blew from the west.

"I'd better get back." Nick scanned the horizon, the setting sun obscured by the boiling clouds. "Christian and I are going to investigate the storm drains before the next cloudburst."

"I've been remiss in not welcoming Christian to our town. I'm curious how he found his way here. Was it the advertising about our growing artists' colony?"

Nick snorted. "Not likely." He glanced at Yancy. "No offense." Nick studied his hands for a moment. "I met Christian when I took shore leave and went hiking in the Aurunci Mountains. I promised Aunt Helen if I ever got to Italy, I'd make the pilgrimage to the Hermitage of San Michel Arcangelo. She'd heard tales as a child of our family climbing to the church as part of a festival."

"Is Christian Italian?"

"No," Nick laughed. "He's from Scotland. He was on a similar journey. We spent three nights camping in the mountains. I invited him to Waterton if he ever visited the US. I didn't expect to be back here so soon or to have him drop in. But here he is."

"I hope he stays … at least, long enough to meet him. Scotland is one of the places I'd love to visit. Triss speaks of the beauty of the country and the warmth of the people." Yancy put a hand on Nick's arm. "Nick, I've met the trolls, the gargoyles and the wererats. But Gino is different." He let the statement hang.

"Full of curiosity today, aren't we?" Nick looked him in the eye. "Do you really want to know?"

"I ... uh ... I do have second thoughts, but I should know. After all, it's a mayor's job to know his constituents. The thing about the pixies and the dirt ..."

"It's soil from his home country. It's a superstition. He needs it to stay ... alive."

"You mean, stay undead, don't you?"

Nick nodded.

"You're not going to tell me anymore, are you?"

Nick shook his head.

Yancy took a deep breath letting it out between his teeth. "Okay, then. I'll add him to my list ... interesting people to get to know. He does make a great dirty martini." He held out his hand. "Thanks for trusting me."

Nick took Yancy's hand and gave it a firm shake. "Glad to have you in our court, Yancy." Turning, he disappeared down the stairs.

Yancy listened to the door close, the lapping waves against the stonewall the only sound for a moment. Staring out over the water at the lights from Professor Lizzard's observatory, he pulled the townsfolk into his heart. "Yep, I liked the open road, a new night ... a new town. But I love this town every night."

Turning his collar up, he strolled down the darkening street, nodding to each individual as they passed.

Chapter Six
*Nick and Christian explore the storm drains
Sherry does the same*

Nick pulled out the knife he kept in his boot. Gino winced at the scraping on the whetstone.

"Goin' out tonight, boss?" Gino focused his attention on washing the beer mugs in the soapy water. Next shift from the docks was due.

"Just downstairs."

"Taking the priest with you?"

"He's not a priest." Nick let another oil droplet fall onto the stone and drew the blade across it.

"Sure smells like one."

"Gino."

Gino jumped at the snarl in Nick's voice.

"Okay, Boss."

The edge sharpened to his satisfaction, Nick descended the back stairs. Christian stood at the bottom, a cross bow nestled in his arm. "Heavy artillery?"

"You weren't there when the buzz saw was in full rotation."

The two men walked through the subway entrance and down the track.

"According to the plans Jonas sent over, the storm sewer system is a level below the subway." Nick visualized the schematic. "The entrance should be somewhere around Third Street." Their footsteps echoed in the tunnel.

"This thing ever work?" Christian surveyed the seating along the wall at the abandoned subway station.

"According to my grandfather's stories, it was a great success for a while. Until it chewed the hairpiece off the mayor's wife's head."

Christian guffawed, the rough sound reverberating. "Hairpiece?"

"Wig. She was completely bald. The wig was human hair sent all the way from France and cost a prince's inheritance. The fan sucked it in and spit out cat fur"

"A little retribution followed?"

"Close to being run out of town on a rail, feathers and all." Nick surveyed the wall to the left. He ran his hand along the brick. A soft spot gave under his fingers. He dug in deeper, found the iron ring and pulled the door open. "Granddad said the engineer went down the Hudson to New York City on a garbage scow. Made a better start there."

Nick descended the stone steps into the darkness. He winced when Christian flipped on the flashlight.

The roar of rushing water drowned out any further conversation. Christian's light hit the muddy surface at the bottom, the beam playing across the fast-moving water sloshing over the channel's edges. Branches, dead rats and other dim objects rolled in the turbulent water pouring from smaller tunnels joining at all angles. A cold breeze blew off the river through the four-foot exit pipe. A large branch draped with grey cloth and refuse half blocked the exit.

Nick motioned to Christian to lean closer. "I'll go up the right branch. You take the left. Shout if you find anything."

"Think you'll hear me over the noise?"

"I'll do my best." Nick took a step toward the pipe. "The pipes become narrower away from the river. Watch the flow. If it rains again, it may get dicey."

"Got it." Christian bent low to enter the narrow tunnel.

Nick watched the water for a few moments. On his first step, his foot slipped on the slime and he went to one knee.

"Damn!"

He fought against the current to get his footing and crept forward, hunched over. He visualized the schematic. In several yards, the pipe connected with a large underground catch basin for the runoff from the zoological park and the residential area. He slogged on until the low ceiling gave way to a taller area. The noise level dropped.

Interesting, the water is warmer here. The air smelled like burnt matches. *Who would be down here?* He amended his thoughts. *Who would need matches?*

Rhythmic sloshing caught his attention. Light bounced up and down from the right-hand tunnel. He stepped back against the brick wall and held his breath. A slight figure emerged into the open area and swept the light around. She sneezed.

"Bless you." Nick murmured.

Sherry whipped around, her arm pulling back. The flashlight shook as she peered into the darkness.

"You!" she shouted. Her word bounced off the walls. She lowered the flashlight but kept Nick's face illuminated. "See? I was right. You did leave without me."

"Only after you didn't return." He smiled at her.

"Liar." She took a step forward. "Do not even for a moment think I need your help. I will handle this swarm by myself."

Nick turned to the opposite tunnel. He flicked on his flashlight and peered into the gloom. Cold water poured from the pipe in a steady stream, the level rising over his boot top.

"How did you get down here?" He swept the room looking for Sherry. She ran her hand along the brick wall on the opposite side.

"I was going to ask you the same. There are two pipes coming into this area and you certainly didn't come down the small one." She went on examining the wall.

"I came up from below. There is an outflow pipe." He took a step forward, noting the increased depth.

"Not one I can find." She stroked the wall. "The wall feels warm, even slightly alive. It is textured, like scales and it has that same smell of burnt matches."

Nick reached her side. He slapped his hand against the wall where he was certain the pipe had been. His palm stung from the contact. Water sloshed around his knees.

"Oh my, these wellies aren't tall enough for this depth." She headed back toward the pipe leading from the zoo. "To answer your question, there is a stair which lets out beside the pipe from the zoo. It was marked on the schematic as a repair access. Apparently, the system clogs up with debris and needs to be cleaned."

"Dr. Ramhill, I think we should consider …" Nick studied the rising water.

"Sherry. Call me Sherry." She ran her hand over the wall again sniffing at it. "I don't recognize the scent but there is definitely sulfur involved. It would account for the poor thing's indigestion and pica."

Nick grabbed her by the shoulders and pushed her gently toward the access from the zoo. "Where are the stairs?" He demanded, the water nearly to his knees and well over her boot tops. She pulled at the leaden wellies unable to make headway against the rushing water.

"Just in here. A few steps." She struggled against the flowing water. Nick picked her up from the water-filled boots and held her close against his chest. He ducked into the smaller tunnel and felt for the opening to the stairs. His hand met the same solid scaly surface.

"Damn! We're cut off."

"Cut off? By whom? Or is it who? I am never certain." Sherry craned around sweeping the flashlight. She turned it toward Nick. His eyes burnt black in this face, no color around the iris. He flinched from the bright light.

He stepped back into the catch basin, the water now to his waist. "Is there another way out?" he shouted above the roaring. "Do you remember the schematic?"

Sherry closed her eyes, pausing for a moment. "No, the only access is the stairs from the zoo. And then the outflow." She squinched her eyes. "Wait, there is a manhole at the top. It is somewhere down the road from Madam Miriam's."

Nick looked up at the ceiling, the manhole outline illuminated by the lightning flashes. "That's over thirty feet." He looked down at the water swirling above his waist. "How well do you swim?"

"Me? Why, I swim just fine, thank you."

"Good." He released her from his arms. She floundered in the water, nearly falling. She grabbed his arm and clung to it.

"Why is the water rising? It should be flowing out to the river." She pulled the sputtering flashlight free from the water. It short circuited and went out.

"Because the access is clogged."

"Then we best go unclog it."

61

Nick grabbed her by the shoulders. "Dr. Ram—Sherry, something is deliberately keeping us in here. It's no coincidence the outflow and the access are both walled in."

"But who … and why?" Her face blanched, her teeth chattering. She stumbled as the flow increased.

He reached under her arm and pulled her tight against his side. The water washed over his head. A circular light flickered at the ceiling. He kicked his feet to stay above water. He rolled Sherry a little higher in his grasp and stared at the dark ceiling willing a repeat flash. Lightning cracked and thunder shook the room simultaneously. The hair on his neck stood up.

"There's the manhole." He pointed at the ceiling with his free hand. "We can tread water until it fills. Another twelve feet, I would guess."

Sherry shivered. "If we have to tread water for very long, I had best take off this boiler suit." She squirmed away, pulling at the zipper. She took a deep breath and dove under. Nick grabbed for her, losing her in the dark water. He swung around as she touched his shoulder.

"Don't do that again!" He growled at her.

She dove away from him. He lunged for her but his hand caught in small branches tangled with garden twine.

"Sherry," he yelled.

> *Nick!* Christian's thoughts rang in his head cutting through the roar.

Nick took two long strokes, gliding until his hands hit the downstream wall. "Christian, we're trapped. The wall, it wasn't there before." He smacked his forehead realizing Christian couldn't hear him.

Okay, Priest, we'll play it your way, he thought. Closing his eyes, he concentrated on Christian's face. *Christian, we're trapped. The water's rising.*

You don't have to shout, Christian responded, a chuckle evident even in his telepathic message. *Stand back.*

Nick felt the wall bulge under his hand. He imagined Christian's punch having experienced it when they sparred. A shiver ran up the wall. Nick glanced back for Sherry. She waved at him from across the space, treading water.

Christian, the water is about ten feet deep and rising. There's a manhole at the top. We're headed up.

He pushed off. The wall shuddered behind him and a crossbow bolt sizzled past his head. "Hey, watch it."

The wall dissolved. Water found a way out, sucking the debris down the pipe. Nick fought the current, searching for Sherry. Her hand hit his shoulder and he grabbed her, the white camisole giving him a target. Securing a handful, he heaved upward, kicking against the current.

Let me break the surface for just one breath, he prayed. The water dragged him backwards into the pipe. He wrapped his arms around Sherry, pulling her head against his chest and rolling to keep her on top. His back scraped the rough brick surface, the pain hissing through him. They slalomed down the pipe.

Nick held Sherry tighter. Suddenly she pushed at him, struggling in his arms.

Air, he thought. *We really need air.* But his lungs weren't burning, the drive to inhale absent. Sherry's struggles weakened. Nick shifted her higher in his grasp, his hand still protecting her head. He pulled her face close, his lips finding hers. He exhaled. She tightened her grip on him, inhaling.

The water's velocity slowed, the level dropping. Nick pushed Sherry up, holding her above the water's surface. He felt her chest heave as she gulped air. His back contacted the rough bottom. Their forward motion ceased. The water rushed past his body, draining away, leaving him lying in the mud.

Sherry twisted around, easing off his chest. She sat back against the brick wall. "Thought for certain we'd end up in the river." She coughed, her voice raspy. "Thanks for the buddy breathing. Have not done that since scuba diving with Uncle Nigel." She coughed again. "He always tasted like spearmint."

"It must have stopped raining." Nick rolled over and pointed down the last length. Lightning flashed, illuminated the raging river beyond. Sherry shivered.

Nick rose, balancing in the slime. He held out a hand to her and pulled her to her feet. Steadying her, he noticed the slim athletic figure. She blushed under his scrutiny. He pulled off his wet coat and draped it around her shoulders.

"Not much for warmth," he murmured. "But it will keep you covered decently. We'd best get back to the bar." He ushered her toward the steep stairs to the subway.

The sound of retching stopped him on the first step. He whipped around, leaving Sherry on the stairs.

"Christian?"

Long fingers and white knuckles clung to the corrugated pipe hanging out over the river. Strangled gasps reached his ears. He grabbed Christian's wrist, hauling him up and into the pipe. Christian hung limp in his grasp, struggling for air. His crossbow dropped from his hand as his eyes rolled back in his head.

Nick laid him out face down on the channel's edge. Wrapping his arms around Christian's chest, he pulled sharply back, forcing air from Christian's lungs. Christian retched, water pouring from his mouth. A second and third squeeze brought more water. Finally, he gasped, his chest shuddering. Nick rolled him over on his back and studied his face. He sighed as Christian's color returned and his eyes opened.

A scream brought them both to their knees. Nick rose and supported Christian as they struggled to his feet.

Sherry stood still, facing them, her eyes rolled up at the ceiling. A tall shadow stood behind her. Long fingers held a red wool blanket in place around her shoulders.

Madrecita chuckled, an earthquake rumble in their ears. She turned Sherry around to face her. Sherry's head tilted up … and then up some more. Deep mahogany eyes looked down at her from Madrecita's seven-foot height. Black hair hung in a long braid across her broad shoulder.

"Lil one, you'll be warmer now." Madrecita patted Sherry on the back. "And you two," She turned blazing eyes on Nick and Christian. "Playing in puddles. Risking the young doctor's life. Shame on you." She draped a long arm around Sherry then looked back at the two men. "Come along. Stew's waiting." Leaning down to Sherry, she murmured, "High time you met my People."

Sherry nodded. Madrecita helped her navigate the steep steps.

"Tsk tsk, no shoes. Marty, come help the doctor."

Marty appeared at Madrecita's side. He held out bright purple knitted slippers. "Thought you'd be about the same size as my darling wife." He helped Sherry balance as she slid into the slippers, a little large but warm and dry. "Now, if those two laggamuffins will hurry up, we'll see about a hot toddy for you."

Chapter Seven

The Mayor returns home

Yancy noted with grim satisfaction the evening sky reflected the murkiness in the bar he'd left behind. "Good. Damn, I sure hope Triss is back." The stately Queen Anne Victorian house inherited from his parents rustled and groaned at night without Triss. Working late and stopping off at the bar was a habit when she was not home to greet him.

Family is important ... to her. His own had been a trial. *Rather boring in truth.* He trudged up the tree-lined lane. *The usual teenage rebellion and nightly fights with an overbearing father. Ho hum.* He shook his head. *How clichéd can life be?*

Yancy pulled open the wrought iron gate. The walkway passed through a wildflower riot holding their heads high against the heavy grayness. He paused, remembering the smile on his wife's face when the tender green sprouts took hold, replacing the manicured lawn with her carefully planned glorious chaos.

Then there is Triss. Her lovely high cheek bones and sea green eyes swam in his vision. "Why in the world did you choose me? I wanted to be a rover and a dreamer with you but you brought me home," he muttered climbing the front steps.

Running off after college—finishing his degree only to stop the fighting with his father—his dream thrived for a while. When he met Triss, she already knew the life on the road and she traveled with him, pulling forth kindness from strangers in town after town. Her smile, laughter and generous heart warmed the cantankerous and curmudgeonly. They were happy on the move.

Until his father's illness. Then she insisted family came first and would not give in until he agreed to return to the river town. Only for a while, he vowed. Only until his father recovered.

So here we are, both of my parents buried. At least, we could be civil at the end. Thanks to Triss.

"But why are we still here?" He addressed the lion door knocker. The smug old face did not answer.

He fit the old key into the antiquated lock. Though aged, the mechanism turned smoothly, and the oak door swung open without protest.

What in the world is wrong with me? I love this house, but I feel like an interloper when Triss isn't here. The old man would laugh to see me the mayor. I'm too naive to be a schemer. Yancy stood in the doorway, the dark foyer looming ahead. *Probably not smart enough, either.*

"But I succeed because Triss really listens … cares enough to put up with my bullshit then helps me state clearly what to do and why. God help me if I don't want to finish the job once I've started. Triss is my true north, but why does she love me?" He leaned his forehead against the doorframe.

"You're tempting the other planes if you stand in the doorway, Yancy."

He jerked to awareness, scanning the shadows in the rooms on either side. "Triss?"

Her lean, supple frame separated from the darkness in the kitchen hall. He felt her open arms pull him. He stepped forward, fighting to unpeel his hands from the doorframe, sensing the pressure trying to hold him back. Feeling her hand on his shoulder, the pull released. He embraced her, holding her tight. Remembered wood fires and sage filling his nose, he inhaled her essence.

"Triss," he spoke into the soft ebony hair draped across her neck and down her shoulder. "I thought you weren't here. You always turn on the lights. The house is so dark."

"Shh, Yancy." She hugged him tighter, her warm breath tickling his ear. "I just arrived." She unwound her arms from his. As she stepped away, he tensed, losing her warmth.

Light flooded the hallway. Yancy squinted, reaching out his other senses to find her. Her soft fingers intertwined with his, and she pulled him toward the kitchen.

"Mother sent treats for you. She remembers how much you like the perogies." She smiled and assumed her mother's larger than life persona. "Tell the skinny boy I will continue to try and make him man-size. He likes my good food, Triss. You should keep him." She dropped his hand and opened the quilted bag on the counter. "She even sent garlic achaar despite Father's objections." She held up a small crock. Opening the lid, Yancy inhaled the pungent spices, clearing his fog.

His mouth watered. He swallowed, tasting the stale gin and his fatigue. *Oh my God, my breath must resemble backwash from Hell.* "Let me clean up. Then I'd love a bite." He kissed her palm echoing the sappy movies his mother had loved. "I'll be right back."

He bounded up the stairs two at a time, chanting *She's home. She's home,* all the way to the master bedroom.

***

Damp hair clinging to his neck, he wiped the plate clean with a sourdough bread morsel. "What a wonderful meal. The best I've had in ... oh, let me see." He watched her eyes glitter at his compliment. "I would say eleven days and...."

He looked at his watch, "Ten hours and fourteen minutes. The last breakfast I had with you before you left." He gazed at her face marveling again this beautiful woman would settle for him.

She smiled, lifting an eyebrow at his unspoken self-judgment. He flushed, unsettled by the feeling she could read his mind.

"Are things well with your family?" He sought a safer subject. "Did you convince them to visit when winter comes?"

"We're still negotiating. You know how Father can be." Triss rose, stacking the plates and turning on the water. Steam curled up from the sink.

How does she get it hot so fast? I have to run it for hours to be tepid. Yancy stood, searching for the towel. Spying it on the rack, he transferred the remaining glassware to the counter and snagged the cloth, ready for the first dish.

"Yeah, but if you've convinced your Mom, I know she'll figure out a way for it to be his great notion." Yancy grabbed the dish she held out and released without looking in his direction.

Triss nodded, humming under her breath.

"My darlin', I'm so glad you're home! Jonas is ready to form a recall committee and I'm not certain he doesn't have a case."

Triss continued washing without comment.

Yancy detailed the day's events outlining the deal too good to pass up. "But the troubling part is they want to build on the zoo property. They say it's the best site for maximum advantage. The tax revenue would be a welcome addition to the budget. You know North Street has potholes to completely swallow your father's wagon … including the mulcs."

Triss laughed. She emptied the dish pan and turned off the light over the sink. He dried the last glass and set it in the cupboard. Turning around, he found the kitchen empty. Smiling to himself, he flicked off the kitchen light and hurried to the living room door.

Triss sat on the floor facing the fireplace nursing a small flame. The scent of apple wood surrounded him. Kneeling beside her, he pulled the brandy decanter from the hearth and poured exactly the expected amount into each snifter. The flames grew steadily. She reached for the snifter, her fingers lingering against his hand.

"Triss. You've hardly said a word. Is everything okay?" His brow wrinkled deeply. He implored her with his eyes.

"Of course, dragă." She leaned forward to graze his lips with her own. "I wished for you to finish your tale."

"I'm so finished!" Yancy flopped on his back, his feet and hands in the air.

"My poor dead bug!" Triss exclaimed and laid alongside him, resting her chin on her elbow and running slender fingers through his hair.

Miasma, if you could teach me to purr, Yancy thought, his mind calming at her touch.

"My turn, then. Mother would gladly accept the warm haven for the winter. She is intrigued by what I've told her about Madam Miriam and would like to know more about her. I only hope Granny is still here when they arrive."

Yancy sighed, his eyes closed, his feet warmed by the fire.

"Da dares not let her stay in one place too long for she does try to put down roots. And ..." she tweaked his nose causing his eyes to fly open. "you're going to be an uncle."

70

"What?" Yancy rolled to his side facing her, his arm around her waist. He rubbed her back in a circle, reveling in the firm muscles.

"Mikal's wife is expecting in November."

"All the more reason for them to come! We've excellent care at the hospital, and if they want nontraditional care, there's Madam Miriam." His eyes sparkled imagining the house filled with voices. Songs and laughter always accompanied Triss' family. "This place has been silent too long."

Triss laughed, pulling his head to her. She kissed him slowly, running her tongue along his lips. When she released him, he gulped the brandy, handing her untouched snifter to her and mimed she should finish it.

He stretched, yawning until his jaw cracked. "Time for bed, mistress." He jumped up, thankful for Jonas' constant yammering about the exercise room in the basement at city hall. Sweeping her from the floor, he set off for the stairs. Her laughter buoyed him as his knees wobbled on the last few steps.

"Tomorrow, I will tell you about the pushy woman who cornered Jonas today. Something about the water damage to the zoo. I thought the place was closed when the old vet died. Wasn't there an investigation?" Before he could go on, Triss slipped from his arms and disappeared into the bedroom.

"Tomorrow." At her word, he forgot all about the zoo, finding only one singular thought in his head.

Chapter Eight
Sherry meets the Troll Clan

Two long shadows behind Madrecita resolved into her husband-brothers. Each held out blankets to Nick and Christian, lending strong arms to support them as they slipped across the muddy floor. The group mounted the stairs in silence. Half a mile along, Madrecita steered Sherry toward a large metal sliding door. Pulling it aside without a sound, they entered a cavernous room ringing with voices and clattering dishes. Warm light suffused the area, radiating from the walls. A roaring fire in the walk-in fireplace added a soothing touch. Heavy iron caldrons simmered over the fire.

"Welcome to our home." Madrecita's deep voice caressed Sherry's ear. "We are a communal people and love to share the hearth with all." She steered Sherry down a side tunnel with curtained doorways. Madrecita pulled back the heavy hanging curtains and ushered Sherry into an alcove. Inside, a deep pile carpet in Middle Eastern patterns covered the floor and rich tapestries hung on the rough stone walls. An ornate, carved cherry chest, taller than Sherry filled one corner. She counted twelve deep drawers. Madrecita pulled open a middle drawer and ran her hands through the silky fabrics.

Sherry studied Madrecita for the first time. *Tall,* she thought, *lean frame with broad shoulders. Strong jaw and broad nose. Platter-sized hands ... but not like Arnie's.* She remembered the sledgehammers Arnie sported. *Not gargoyle. Oh my, troll?*

"Valley." Madrecita held out a skirt in deep sapphire and matching tunic. The fabric shimmered, shot through with silver thread. "Valley troll, dear. We're thinner and lighter boned than our mountain cousins. Europe is overrun with the mountain trolls which keeps my people in the shadows. Your textbooks would not mention us."

"Are you reading my mind?" Sherry stared at her.

"No, not at all. I leave that to Miasma. Just guessing the questions an intelligent young woman would ask." She laughed, the rumble echoing off the high ceiling. "Now, you may find this more comfortable than those wet things. These were my daughter's. They should fit you."

"Were?" Sherry looked down. "I am so sorry. What happened to her?"

"She grew up." Madrecita split the curtains, her chuckle vibrating in the still air. "There is water in the basin and small clothes in the bottom drawer. Feel free to take whatever fits you. Dinner's ready."

Rushed to judgment again, didn't you? You really must stop. She shed the wet clothes and scrubbed her skin to glowing with a cloth, drying with the heavy blanket. The lowest drawer revealed cotton underwear, the fabric as fine as silk. She pulled on the skirt and slipped the tunic over her head, reveling in the comforting feel. She twirled, wishing for a mirror. Smoothing the front, she stepped toward the curtain.

Ahem. Miasma untangled from the luxurious covers on the bed.

Sherry spun around at the sound. *Miasma, should you be here?*

I may be where ever I am. She washed a front paw then turned green orbs on Sherry. *Your hair.*

She ran her fingers through her hair. *Oh my. It must be a fright.*

She spied a comb by the water basin. Fingering it, she wondered if Madrecita would mind. Deciding her hostess would most likely not, she ran it through her hair pulling small twigs and leaves from the tangles. *Oh, my. I am glad I do not have a mirror.*

Clattering silverware on pottery reached her ears setting off a rumble in her stomach. *Must be nearly nine. Elegant time to dine.* Satisfied her hair was at least presentable, she slipped the knitted slippers back on and hurried down the tunnel.

As many as thirty large individuals sat at the long dining table. Men and women alike were dressing in heavy overalls and denim shirts. Cascades of long silky hair poured down the backs of the women while the men sported short cuts of curly hair.

Through the double doors at the end of the chamber, Sherry could see another long table but this one was occupied by a mixture of men, women and children all dressed in vibrant colors, tunics and pants, flowing dresses and elegant vests. Laughter filled the air.

A huge male sat at the far end of the table dwarfing his companions. Sherry stepped forward, searching for a place. The man rose, towering twice her height. He patted the empty chair on his right. "Honored guest, here is your place." Sherry barely discerned the nearly subsonic tones in his voice. He beckoned to her. She scanned the table finally finding Christian, his fair hair freshly washed and glinting in the candlelight. Ten candelabras lit the table. Fine crystal filled with amber liquid shone in the flickering light. She arrived at her place and her host pulled out her chair. He offered her a hand as she climbed onto the tall chair.

"I feel like Alice in Wonderland. Thank you." She smiled at him.

He half bowed. "I am Gregariel, but please call me Greg. Welcome to our clan."

"Thank you." Sherry glanced down the table locating Nick in a dark space between the pools of candlelight. He chatted with his neighbor while scraping the bottom of the soup bowl with thick, whole grain bread.

"Forgive our lack of manners but Madrecita suggested you would be more comfortable if everyone was not waiting impatiently. The clan members at this table must move along soon. I promise, there is plenty left for you." Proving his point, he picked up a coffee can-sized ladle and spooned a generous portion into her bowl.

The aroma of the roasted vegetables sent saliva squirting through her mouth. She touched her lips with the damask napkin.

"It's vegetarian." Greg leaned close keeping his voice low. "The trencher in the middle has venison if you wish but many here do not eat flesh." He smiled revealing large sharp canines.

Sherry filled her spoon. Fine herbs and a rich broth brought a sigh. She concentrated on the thick stew, savoring each legume and vegetable. When the ache in her stomach subsided, she paused and looked around. Greg smiled at her again and handed her the hot dinner rolls. A small crock filled with honey butter followed.

Sherry felt Greg's eyes on her as she finished a second roll slathered in butter. Her mind whirled with questions. "Where are they going?" She swept her hand at the table.

"They're soon off to work."

"Oh, you mean the Midnight Crew."

Greg laughed deep in his chest. "That is a title Nick provided us. It means all of us here." He glanced at the other room. "But it is accurate for those at this table tonight. They are working the midnight shift on the docks."

Sherry noted the mix of men and women.

"Yes, our women work as hard … if not harder … as our men. They can do anything on the docks." He handed Sherry a third roll. She took it without hesitation. "It's good to see you with an appetite. Too many young women eat less than nothing." Greg patted her on the back. "I like you."

Sherry smiled at him. "Thank you. I like you, too. I assume you are the clan leader."

Greg guffawed. "No, little sister. Madrecita is Clan Mother. She is the true leader. I'm her husband. The scrawny bloke sitting beside her is my husband-brother."

"Husband-brother? Scrawny?" She wrinkled her brow, staring at the tall young troll with dark hair and vivid green eyes seated at Madrecita's left. She estimated his shoulders to be three feet across.

"We're a matriarchal people. The women understand the need for diversity in the population so they can take as many husbands as they choose. As First Husband, she confers with me as I must accept the next one as my brother."

"How long have you been in Waterton?"

"Three generations." Greg offered her another roll. She shook her head. "My great grandfather came to this country to work on the whaling ships. When he had enough saved, he brought my great grandmother from Andalusia. She was so seasick on the way over, she refused to live by the coast so upriver was the compromise." He chuckled. "She was pregnant with my grandmother and to this day, my grandmother won't eat fish."

"Your grandmother is still here, too? But I don't see anyone over 40 at the table." Sherry looked around, using both senses of sight.

"We are a long-lived species." He nodded toward the table in the other room. "She is overseeing the others. The children adore her." Greg passed a dish overflowing with honeyed almonds. "I keep the bees," he said, looking down at his plate.

Sherry bit into the treat, savoring the mild orange flavor. Greg did not look up. Sherry realized he waited for approval and laid her hand on his arm. He glanced at her, eagerness in his eyes.

"They are wonderful. Where is your apiary?"

"In the zoo." He held out the bowl again and she took several more.

"I am seriously showing my ignorance. I thought I had walked most everywhere in the zoo. I do not remember seeing any beehives."

"They aren't traditional hives. The bees live in the aviary … in the walls." Greg looked to the far end and nodded when Madrecita raised her hand. "The orange flavor is from the orange trees in the simian compound. Now, if you'll excuse me, I'll fetch coffee. Then it is off to work."

"Are you nocturnal?"

Greg chuckled, grinding gravel to her ears. "No more than you, little sister." He waved his arm at the folks lining the table. "Can you imagine all these folks being seen in daylight?"

"Yes, I can." Sherry straightened her spine and stuck out her chin. "I can and it is not fair you should have to stay hidden. You should be able to walk about any time you wish."

"Thank you, little sister, for your concern. But we are happy." He glanced down the table. "My Clan Mother wishes to speak with you." He gave Sherry a hand to help her slip off the tall chair.

Sherry walked the thirty feet, nodding to individuals as they rose and deposited dishes in large pans. Each held gallon canisters for hot coffee. Greg stood by the door, filling each from a twenty-gallon pot.

Male and female alike, they filed out into the subway tunnel. Greg's husband-brother gathered up the dishes and juggled them while pulling out the chair for Sherry. He smiled, not meeting her eye. She judged him several years younger than Greg.

"Come, barkeep." Greg called from the door. "I'll walk with you." He patted a large pouch at his waist. "I wish to settle the clan tab."

Nick rose, deposited his dishes in the receptacle and bowed to Madrecita. Before he could speak, she addressed him. "Marty will escort the good doctor home when we're done."

Dismissed, he nodded to Sherry and disappeared into the dark tunnel. Sherry looked around, realizing Christian was already gone but Marty sat on a high barstool at Madrecita's side.

Madrecita poured three pottery mugs with the rich dark coffee and added brandy to each. She offered one to Sherry who took it and savored the first sip. "We have already sent word to Madam you are safely with us."

"Thank you for your kindness," she addressed Madrecita. "You are most gracious to share your table with me." Her face burned. "And for correcting my rudeness to not think to let Madam know of my whereabouts."

"You are important to us, Dr. Ramhill." She looked at Marty. "To all here."

"Please, call me Sherry. Dr. Ramhill is … oh, there are many in my family and I do not stand on ceremony." Sherry took another sip, the warmth spreading lassitude through her stiff muscles. Her scrapes and bumps nagged a little now that other concerns had been addressed.

"We are worried. Dr. Alighieri said the zoological garden was under attack."

Sherry sat up straight, sleep banished. "Attack? How? By whom?"

Marty sat forward, his face shining in the light. "From several directions, Doctor … Sherry. First, there is the water issue."

"Oh, yes. Something definitely did not want us in the catch basin." Sherry shivered, remembering the terror. "Or rather wanted to keep us there."

Marty nodded. "Dr. Alighieri was investigating a presence when he died. But more than that, there's a developer who wishes to buy the zoo property. He claims it will bring new revenue to the city. At the very least, it will be taxable property."

"That certainly fits with the dossier on the Mayor's desk." Sherry finished the coffee, suppressing a yawn.

"We have kept you too long after your ordeal." Madrecita patted her hand. "We need to confer on both issues. My people count on the zoo property for a large portion of our existence."

Sherry stared at her.

"I am certain my darling husband shared with you his passion for the bees."

Sherry nodded.

79

"There are other things we grow on the zoo grounds … always sharing with the animals. Buffalo chips are wonderful fertilizer." She smiled at Sherry as the second yawn rolled across her face. "But now, little one, let Marty conduct you home. I will arrange with my fellow sisters and we will all talk during the daylight hours."

Marty leapt off his stool and hurried to offer Sherry his hand. Her knees gave a little when her feet contacted the ground and he held her up.

"But these clothes … and my clothes?" She shook her head to clear her heavy eyelids.

"That outfit looks wonderful on you. I wish you to keep it." Madrecita draped an arm around her shoulder and steered her toward the door. "Your own things will be laundered and returned to you. Perhaps we will also find your Wellingtons. Our little ones are excellent scavengers and will be excited to search for treasure along the river bank after the rain. Now off with you." She turned a dark eye on Marty.

He placed a finger on his nose and winked. "Now, Madrecita, I will see the good doctor safely home and into Miasma's care." Marty offered Sherry his arm.

"Thank you, dear friend."

Sherry leaned on Marty. Her feet were leaden, and she dreaded the long walk back to the zoo. She opened her eyes wide as Marty directed her to a golf cart parked in a side tunnel. He chuckled. She fell asleep before the cart rolled ten yards.

Chapter Nine

Jonas gets a workout

Jonas rubbed his face and shook himself awake. He walked down the stairs to the basement gymnasium. Though an early riser, six a.m. still took him by surprise. He needed a good workout before he took on the Mayor over the complex paperwork in the proposal. Inconsistencies itched at his mind along with a nasty suspicion someone was trying to railroad this proposal through without proper review. He just couldn't get the pieces to fit … yet.

Clacking wood on wood stopped him before he opened the fire door. Few people had access to the city hall before opening hours and they were not the type to be using the gym equipment. Even security was not available at the moment. He'd seen Sinclair running to the donut shop—the only running the overweight guard ever did—assuming no one would be around to notice his absence.

Jonas gripped his gym bag and swung open the door. He jumped into the room prepared to use the bag as a weapon. "Ah ha!" he shouted.

Nick checked his blow in midstroke when Christian turned toward Jonas. The two men held long wooden rods. Barefoot, they stood on the sparring mats, both dripping sweat down bare chests. Opposites, Nick's black hair hung loose on his shoulders, a leather headband holding it out of his face, while Christian's fair hair was tightly braided into a queue. Christian laid the staff on the floor near a long sword.

Nick leaned on his, pulling a sweat rag from his waistband and wiping his face.

"Uhhh, I don't mean to interrupt." Jonas stammered.

"Jonas, not to worry. Why dinna you join us?" Christian picked up a water bottle and downed the contents.

"I just came down to use the elliptical. I didn't realize anyone was in the gym at this hour of the morning." Jonas edged around the mat toward the stationary equipment.

"Morning? Is it morning?" Christian chuckled. "We were just finishing the night." He flipped the quarterstaff up with his foot and caught it in one hand. "Ever try these?"

"Uhhh, no." Jonas looked from man to man.

Nick took the gym bag from his hand and tossed it on the bench. "Might as well give in, Jonas. When Christian gets that look in his eye, you won't be able to talk him out of it." He nudged Jonas to the mat and pushed him down to a seated position. "Stretch first, though or you'll regret it."

Before Jonas could respond, Nick leapt over him and swung at Christian's head. Christian ducked, turning in a circle and aiming for Nick's knees. Nick dove over the swing, rolling to his feet and jabbing at Christian's midsection. Christian blocked, levering his staff upward and forcing Nick back on his heels. Nick dropped the quarterstaff and, covering his head with both arms, rolled out flat on the mat.

Christian punched his quarterstaff into Nick's sternum.

"Oooof."

"You're getting faster, Nick." Christian offered him a hand. Nick waved him away and crab-walked off the mat.

"I'll stay right here while you teach the pup some basics." He snagged his own bag and sought out the water bottle.

Pup? Jonas thought. He did not have time to contemplate the appellation as Nick flipped his quarterstaff to him. He grabbed for it, missing and sending it clattering across the floor. He jumped up and chased it before either man could criticize him. Holding the staff in both hands, he faced Christian. "Are you sure this is a good idea?"

"For me, yes. For you, perhaps not. But it is long past time you started training." Christian held up his staff. "Your hands should be opposite grips. Are you right or left-handed?"

"Left-handed, sir." Jonas looked down.

"Good." Christian switched his grip on the staff.

"Good? No one's ever said that before." Jonas stared at him. "Especially at school."

"Old way of thinking. Someone who uses the left is very dangerous for someone who has trained only with right-handed opponents." Christian bent his knees and swung the staff in a figure eight. "Okay, I am ready."

"You just changed your grip."

"I did. What is it the Americans call someone who bats with either hand ... a switch-hitter?"

Jonas chuckled, "Be careful using switch hitter anywhere but in a baseball stadium."

Christian raised an eyebrow and glanced at Nick.

Nick laughed. "I'll explain it to you, later. Jonas, grab near the end of the staff with your right hand, thumb down. Then place your left hand near the middle, thumb up. Otherwise, he'll knock it out of your hand on the first swing."

Jonas fumbled with the staff.

"Believe me, I know from experience." Nick rose, stretched his back, and settled on the bench along the wall.

Christian aimed a sideways blow at Jonas. Jonas pushed his own staff to the side and blocked, the clack echoing in the gym. He dropped the staff and blew on his palms.

"Stings, doesn't it?" Christian flipped the fallen staff in the air.

Jonas caught it without thinking. Christian looked at Nick with a slight smile on his face.

"Again," he swung at Jonas' knees. Jonas copied Nick's maneuver and jumped over, landing on his toes and swinging around. Christian blocked the swing.

"Good. Now, let's try some simple drills for footwork."

***

An hour later, Jonas stood under the scalding water in the locker room shower, his shoulders on fire. *Why me?* As the water ran over his head and down his shoulders, he remembered sneaking into his father's study when he was barely five. The closet where his father kept his handgun was open and he peeked around the corner wanting a glimpse. Until now, he didn't know what the wooden poles hanging on the wall were ... had even forgotten noticing them in his quest for the revolver.

His father walked into the room and caught him. He set Jonas on his office desk, tapped him on the nose and said, "Not yet, son. But in due time." Then he hoisted him into his arms and carried him to bed. His father didn't come home the next day.

Jonas felt his eyes burning and he scrubbed at them with his fists. Standing in the shower, he let the water pour over his head and down his face until his breathing quieted.

I wonder if they're still in the closet? He finished his shower and trudged up the stairs to open the office.

Looking at his desk, papers neatly stacked, pencils and pens carefully tucked away, the order seemed odd to him … as if a desire for chaos had crept in with the tingling blows from Christian's staff. He sighed, rolled his shoulders anticipating the stiffness to come. He filled the coffee pot with water.

For the next hour, he poured through the city reports, wishing the Mayor would arrive. He resisted the urge to look at the clock. He hoped to discuss the Santos proposal before the City Council meeting but Yancy held management by walking around as a gospel. Jonas knew he would come in when he had spoken with everyone on his internal list. He shrugged and picking up the tallest stack, opened the spreadsheet to catalogue the property transfers within city limits. Next, he'd tackle the requests for zoning variances. *A college degree for this?*

Just before noon, his cell phone buzzed in his pocket.

***

"Jonas, thanks for coming over on such short notice. Triss and I really appreciate this. I want to run some ideas by you before I meet with the council and hope you'll identify any objections they could possibly raise." Yancy paced around his living room combing fingers through his hair and pulling out his cell phone. He gazed at the text message, snorted, then cursed under his breath. Triss handed him a coffee mug and adjusted his tie.

"Yes, sir, I have the agenda for today's meeting. The board seems eager to get moving on fixing the water problems." Jonas pulled out his notepad but put it away at a shake from Triss. He sat down in the overstuffed loveseat. Triss smiled and handed him a plate.

Drink? She mouthed.

Ginger ale, please, he replied similarly.

"Well, I've a problem with this proposal. They want to take the land from the zoo and develop it into an exclusive resort ... make this town into an expensive get-away for folks from Boston and the City. Not my idea of a way to build our town into a desirable place to live. We have something here which is truly unique and wonderful. To throw it away to increase our tax base is ridiculous and belittles our investment in the future." He glanced over and saw Triss' mouth quirking.

"Okay, I need to be politic. Jonas, what's the best thing you remember about the zoo?"

"You know, I haven't been here very long, but I love we have to reach it by water. It makes it a special day to ride along the river."

"So, if we were to ... I don't know ... um ... copy Providence, for example, and have fund raising events where gondolas take people over for concerts at the zoo. Do you think we could highlight its uniqueness ... and raise funds, too? Not only to cover the repairs but the upkeep as well?" Yancy rocked up and down on heel and toes.

"Well, sir, might be an interesting start, but the cost of the repairs is quite daunting. No one wants to create new taxes or set the city up for a new bond."

"Yes, but we do have quite a few artists and creative types who wouldn't mind some recognition. What about the cute girl from the Courier who's always bugging you to come up with something interesting to report on from the Mayor's office. I mean, c'mon, Jonas, what could be more interesting than cute and cuddly elephants which might be homeless because the mean and nasty Council just wants to add condos?" Yancy paused, his finger in the air. "And increase the City's liabilities due to the need for additional fire and police protection for housing which is available only by water?" Yancy was in top form with his grin on full range devastation.

Triss chuckled.

"Sir?" Jonas' voice held excitement. "I love the idea but what about the access road running along the ridge. There was something about it in the property transfers this morning … I didn't remember until now."

"Of course, I didn't forget but I hope the council members have. We'll look at what you found after the meeting." He smiled his great smile at Jonas. "What else?"

"Mrs. Kent—you know, at Granny's Attic on Baker Street—told me the Pierces were the last couple to have a wedding ceremony at the zoo back in 1968. The City Council was furious because the wedding party was barefoot and the ladies in the wedding party weren't wearing bras by the end. They burned 'em."

Yancy choked. "Cynthia?" He shook the image from his head.

Jonas nodded. "The Council disallowed any more such events. I bet if you suggested there should be private functions at the zoo again, she'd get behind it."

"All the people," Yancy announced. "I know the different folks work at the zoo—at least part time—helping with the animals and the landscaping, especially the heavy tasks. It won't do to take away their livelihood."

Triss pulled Yancy's attention. He looked at her.

"Some councilmen don't wish to acknowledge their existence. You may not win support by bringing them up."

"But maybe it's time they opened their eyes." Yancy puffed up his chest. He glanced at her, jumping when Miasma appeared from behind her. The cat glared at him.

"Now you sound like the new zoo director." Triss smiled.

"I do?" Yancy tore his eyes away from Miasma and his chest deflated.

"Yes, at least what Madam Miriam shared with me yesterday. She's a firebrand for their civil rights."

"And for fixing the storm drain system," Jonas added.

"But this proposal would eliminate the zoo. I don't care they promise to 'preserve' it. That will be cut from phase one, I'm certain. Too expensive." Yancy wiped his face with his hand. "But we have to fix the drainage, or the zoo is in danger anyway." Yancy flopped into the club chair. He reached for his mug and frowned when he found it empty.

Triss held up Yancy's Inverness cape. "You'll be late if you don't start out."

"I remember. It's Markus Whitmore!" Jonas burst out. "He's bought several properties along the back road to the zoo."

"That property is relatively worthless. It's only zoned rural."

Jonas shrugged.

"I doubt he is interested in farming. Very odd." Yancy heaved himself up, straightened his shoulders and accepted Triss' help to don the coat. She handed him an umbrella. The two men stepped out into the rain.

***

Dr. August Ambruson entered the council chamber in the city hall and wrinkled his nose. Already seated at the ornate table, Mrs. Pierce held her handkerchief to her face.

"I do hope the agenda is short today, August. The stench is overwhelming." She put down the cloth and shuffled the papers on the table.

"I most certainly agree, Cynthia. This situation must be addressed and quickly." August sat in his position next to the middle chair. "And I also hope the Mayor will be on time … for once." He put his briefcase on the desk and pulled out the thick sheath comprising the proposal from Santos Development Group.

Miriam DeMarco swept into the room, her regal stature unbowed by the pouring rain. Cynthia noticed her feet weren't even wet and wondered once again about this unusual woman. Cynthia's own mother told stories about Madam Miriam as she was known about town, stories dating back to when her mother was a little girl. But Cynthia's 90-year-old mother had been losing her mind for several years.

Professor Lizzard appeared next, the rain dripping from his long fingers as he closed the umbrella and stepped into the council chamber. He smiled at each one in turn and took his place at the far end from Madam Miriam.

"Only two more to go," muttered August, "and once again the Mayor will be the last."

Cynthia hid her smile, knowing August looked forward to chastising the Mayor for any small infraction … and the Mayor's chronic tardiness was a ripe target. She heard him huff as Jonas held the door open for the remaining two council members and Yancy. She glanced at the clock over the door. The hands stood at one fifty-nine.

"Well, at least, we can start on time this week." Cynthia stole August's thunder. She nodded to the last arrivals.

"Now, Cynthia," Abigail Warren slid by to take her seat next to her. She patted Cynthia's hand. "We all know you're in hurry to get home to your handsome husband."

Cynthia glared at her and remained silent.

Markus Whitmore, council chair, called the meeting to order. He shuffled the papers on the desk. "Now, in light of the weather and as we all know there has been no progress on a solution to the water crisis, I'm using my prerogative to delay all other items to the next agenda and focus on this one item … the proposal from the Santos Development Group."

Yancy rose from his seat. "I think we need to have a thorough discussion of this proposal and the impact on—"

"Mr. Mayor, you are in violation of Robert's Rules of Order. There cannot be discussion until a motion is made. Do I have a motion?"

August shot up, knocking his chair over. "I move the Council accept the proposal from the Santos Development Corporation effective immediately!"

Professor Lizzard raised his hand. "Second."

"Then the proposal is now on the table for discussion." Markus looked at everyone except Yancy.

Abigail raised her hand. "To be brief, we all know the situation. This proposal will be good for the town. I'm in favor."

Professor Lizzard caught Markus' eye. "Professor?"

"The Santos proposal is ambitious, to say the least, and includes losing the town's prized possession ... the zoo." Lizzard continued over the mumbling of the council members. "It would be a travesty. In addition, I'm concerned an upscale resort on the site will reduce the town itself into merely tourist industry."

"Professor," August started.

"August, please wait to be recognized." Markus banged the gavel on the desk.

August's ruddy face deepened.

"Councilman Ambrusen is recognized."

"I would hope so. You've known me for thirty years."

"Jonas, please strike his comment." Markus directed.

"Very well," August gained control. "Professor, a resort hotel or, as they say, a 'destination' would bring jobs to the town. Even before the opening, it would pour money into the

90

building industry which is failing as badly as the sewers." He flipped through the thick proposal. "And here on page 97, they clearly state that the zoo would be maintained as part of the attraction of the property."

Yancy rocked back and forth on his heels. Markus sighed. "Mr. Mayor, do you have comments to add to this discussion?"

"I do." He looked at the council members seated at the table. "I have my concerns about a promise to maintain the zoo. You all know it is an expensive ..." Yancy cleared his throat and pulled on his tie.

Cynthia smirked. *Almost walked into that pit, didn't you, Mr. Mayor.*

Yancy took a deep breath. "What I mean to say is the zoo, as well as other locations in this town and county, provide homes and livelihoods to many different townsfolk." Madam Miriam nailed him with her eyes. He stopped in mid breath.

"Ah ... we have a diverse population both in age and background—"

"Yancy, get to the point." Markus fumed.

"Well, eh, Mrs. Pierce, you recognize how important the zoo is to this town. I'm told your wedding was a magnificent affair. The site must hold sentimental value for you."

Mrs. Pierce snorted. "I should have had an affair with the bastard instead of marrying him. Sentimental value, my ass."

Markus slammed the table with the gavel. "I'm calling the question. All those in favor, please raise your hand."

Four hands went up. Madam Miriam and Professor Lizzard stared at each other from across the table, their hands in their laps.

"Very well, as there seems to the potential for only two negative votes, the motion passes. Mr. Mayor, please inform the Santos group they can begin phase one. With no further business, and hearing the thunder, I adjourn the meeting." Markus snapped his briefcase shut, snatched up his raincoat and hurried to the door.

Yancy stood still. "But we just hired a new Director for the Zoo. It may put the young woman out of a job."

Markus froze in the doorway. He took his time turning. "You what? Without Council approval?"

"It's a staff job. It doesn't require council approval." Yancy gritted his teeth.

"Who interviewed her?" Markus demanded.

"I did." Madam rose to her full height and gathered her coat. "She is eminently qualified." She glided to the door ending the conversation, her face still as stone. Markus stepped aside allowing her to pass. Cynthia followed in her wake, whispering to Abigail.

Yancy let out his held breath.

Professor Lizzard patted him on the back. "We'll find another way, dear fellow. We will, indeed."

***

Yancy handed the umbrella to Jonas. "I'll meet you back at the office." He stepped out into the drizzle and walked along the sidewalk toward the town square. Markus scurried ahead on the pavement and, fumbling with his keys, disappeared into his jewelry store. The door automatically locked behind him.

Yancy paused at Granny's Attic across the street, his back to the jewelry store. The light from it reflected in Granny's display window. Markus moved around, adjusting various displays then sat at his workstation. Yancy turned his collar up and crossed to the door. He pressed the bell and waited for the buzzer indicating the lock had been released.

"Mr. Mayor, is it time for a gift for your lovely wife?" Markus set his jeweler's loop on the counter.

"Markus, it's always time for a gift for Triss but that's not what I'm here about. And it's Yancy. I don't care for the title."

Markus straightened the black silk pad on the glass display case. "I rather enjoyed the formality when I held the office. And if you're here about the Council decision, they voted. Besides it's a good offer."

Yancy stuck his hands in his pocket. "For whom, Markus?"

"Whatever do you mean? For the town … for the folks looking for work." Markus wiped the counter with a cloth. "Can't keep the fingerprints off, you know." He did not look up but scuttled down the length of the display case.

"Markus, there are property transfer forms in my office for the lots along the easement … with your fingerprints on them." Yancy stepped sideways, keeping opposite Markus.

Markus looked up, glaring at Yancy. "There's nothing illegal about buying land. Besides, I have the money."

"I know you have significant means but those lots are not zoned for any development. Seems like a strange purchase."

"Maybe I'm going to run some cattle up there." Markus did not meet Yancy's eye. "Besides, zoning laws can be changed."

"How long have you known about this proposal?" Yancy felt the pulse in his left temple as he tried to keep his voice even.

"I don't care for what you are insinuating, Mr. Mayor. I don't care if you are the mayor, get out." Markus pointed at the door, his hand trembling.

"Markus, if I find out … I'll expect you to step down as chair."

"Wouldn't you like that? I'm the only one holding you back from all your fancy dreams to fill the streets with vagrants. Artists, my ass! This was a nice, quiet town under my care. Now the shop signs go up one week and down the next. Half the storefronts on the block are vacant. And Granny's. She moves in and moves out every time the wind changes direction." His face bloomed bright red, sweat popping out on his forehead. "Like some ancient Mary Poppins."

"Easy, Markus. I'm not here to fight … just wanting to understand the rush on this proposal." Yancy took a step back, giving Markus more room.

"The Council made the decision. And there's nothing you can do to change it."

Yancy took his hand from his pocket and stuck it out toward Markus. Markus flinched back, staring at him. Yancy waited. Markus slowly took the hand. Yancy gave it a firm shake.

"You may be right, but I can try. Have a nice day." He turned on his heel and left the shop.

Chapter Ten

The Ladies meet, Sherry fights the Pink Slip and the Mayor receives Madam Miriam

The private dining room at the Waterline Bar buzzed with quiet conversation. Sherry stared at the remnants of the fine food, once again amazed at the elegance found within the rough and tumble bar. Micah removed the last plate and closed the oak doors behind him. With his exit, Madrecita stood and motioned Sherry to join her at the head of the table.

"Ladies." Madrecita made eye contact with each person … Anastasia representing the wererats, Chazel with her gargoyle wings carefully tucked away to give her luncheon partner elbow room, and, seated on the table top, Maribelle representing the pixie fae clan, her glowing, emerald wings quivering.

Madrecita's expression impressed upon them the gravity of this discussion. "I hope you have enjoyed our luncheon but now, I need you to consider the situation we face. Professor Lizzard has shared his results." She nodded in Sherry's direction. "He's grateful for Dr. Ramhill's timely and valuable assistance."

Sherry felt the color rising in her face as a quiet applause broke out.

"From the data, he concludes a demonic presence—of significant magnitude—has taken up residence in the river valley. However, there is no evidence a major portal from the demonic world exists. If it is a demon, then she—or he—has come here from somewhere else on this plane or the portal has subsequently closed. Dr. Alighieri, most likely, perished from overexposure to brimstone while investigating."

Rumbling broke out around the table. Maribelle's wings quivered so fast she rose several inches in the air. Anastasia patted Chazel's hand stopping her from rising.

"Dr. Alighieri … Dante … was a good man. He didn't deserve such a fate." Chazel dabbed at her eyes with a napkin.

Madrecita held up her hand and waited for silence. "I share your feelings. He was a valued colleague and a dear friend. His demise warns us any actions undertaken by our friends and family must be done with caution."

"What are we going to do?" Chazel looked around the table. Heads nodded in agreement with her inquiry.

"Dr. Ramhill, I believe you're prepared to answer that question." Madrecita handed the ceremonial mace to her. The large wooden talking stick landed heavily in her hands and she staggered back from the table a step. Righting herself, she cradled it in her arms, heat rising in her face at the smiles behind hands and napkins.

"There are a few avenues we can pursue. First, we need to identify the entity … cautiously. While it could be a demon, there is also the possibility it might be a wyrm or young drake. Warm brimstone is their preferred method to heat a bed."

"Dr. Ramhill, what about the creature Christian brought from the river?" Madrecita's clan sister asked.

"A *teppich*. I won't bore you with the scientific description. Under normal circumstances, they are herbivores—plant eaters—much like the manatee in this country. But they are easily addicted to brimstone. When they are afflicted, they will eat most anything and can be quite dangerous, particularly in large numbers. Remove the brimstone and they will go back to their normal feeding grounds."

The double doors slammed aside. Heads turned. Marty jumped up on the table and whispered in Madrecita's ear. He leapt back across the room and closed the doors with a bang.

"Ladies, the Mayor just announced an agreement with a company which will repair the sewer and storm drainage system in exchange for property on which to build a resort hotel. The Council has approved the agreement by a vote of four to two. Sufficient to prevent the Mayor from breaking any tie."

Where? Where? issued from several mouths.

"The zoo." Madrecita sat down, her face grey. A collective murmur washed over the room. The room remained silent for several heart beats. Each woman looked to another for reassurance.

Madrecita stood again, her jaw set. "They will begin phase one this week which means poking around the zoo and most likely the tunnels. It's imperative we move our families farther into the caves. We can't afford to be discovered. Everyone knows their part in the evacuation protocol. Please go and be safe. Report any problems through Anastasia's family. They will be available to your call." She looked at Anastasia who nodded.

At her last word, all stood and cleared the room.

"Well," Sherry stamped her foot. "Just wonderful. Here I am to lead the charge, and I am getting sacked!" She grabbed Madrecita's hand. "I am not giving up on this." She tucked her bumbershoot under her arm and ran for the stairs.

***

"When, exactly, was I going to be notified I am unemployed?" Sherry raised her foot, then thought twice. It was Madam Miriam she was confronting after all.

"Exactly when?" Madam raised an eyebrow as she sipped her tea. She looked over the cup rim at Sherry. "When you *actually* see the proverbial pink slip. The last I am aware you're still the Director."

"But there isn't going to be any zoo." Sherry flopped into the wingback chair and fought to keep the whine from her voice.

"Young woman, sit up." Madam set her teacup and saucer aside. "A lady maintains perfect posture at all times and under any duress." She poured a cup and held it out to Sherry.

Sherry sat up straight and accepted the cup. Madam took a sip, then another. "First, they are promising that the zoo will be maintained as part of the appeal of the complex. Yancy seems to believe they will renege on the agreement. I concur and I, for one, do not intend to let the zoo go without a fight." She raised an eyebrow at Sherry. "And I would certainly hope any niece of Agatha's would have sufficient steel in her spine to help me."

"Of course, I do … will." Sherry burst out, nearly dropping the Royal Albert teacup in her lap.

"Exactly what I expect from you." Madam took the cup from Sherry's hand. "Now, we need a plan. I assume Madrecita has activated the disaster protocol to move the families deeper into the tunnels."

Sherry nodded.

"Excellent. The first phase is expected to take a week. They will send in surveyors, engineers and assorted others to poke around the zoo and the sewer and drainage systems throughout the town. I also assume you have been thorough and know the access to the living sites for our friends." Madam waited for Sherry's response.

"Madam, I will say I have found many, but I will not assert I have found them all. However, I am certain Micah will help me … now something is more important than his games." Sherry frowned remembering the merry chase Micah led her on to find the ones she could now identify.

Madam chuckled. "Micah does love his diversions. But you are correct, he will be a great help. I would suggest to the Director she move the more dangerous animals into compounds where those entrances are found. Then be certain to dog every step those fellows take."

Sherry opened her mouth to tell her few animals were truly dangerous. Even the stately lion was elderly and had few teeth but then she thought about Mistress Wolverine and Billy Boy. *It just might work.*

> *Of course, it will work. I will make it so.* Miasma washed her paw with short wipes. *I will impress upon them the importance. You'll be surprised how fierce they can seem.*

> *Seem is the right word.* Sherry laughed under her breath.

Miasma echoed the sentiment. She disappeared, grey stripes last.

Madam raised an eyebrow, her mouth quirking up. "I see you have your troops mustered. Best get busy." She rose from her chair. "I will see to the other fronts … especially the Mayor. Girding the loins, you know." She smiled at Sherry. "Do be home for dinner. Cook is rather testy. She has been working so hard and you are not here to appreciate her efforts."

"Yes, Madam, I will." Sherry left by the garden door and hurried down the path.

Micah stood waiting at the bottom, a rope looped around Billy Boy's neck.

***

"Madam Miriam, welcome to my office." Yancy stood, smoothing out his vest. "Please have a seat. Jonas, bring Madam Miriam tea."

Madam sat in the library chair next to Yancy's desk. "Thank you, no. This is not a social call. Jonas, you best stay. If you don't mind, your Honor."

Yancy nodded to Jonas. "Of course not. Jonas is a trusted assistant and friend." He sat back in his swivel chair. Jonas pulled up a straight back chair and took out his digital recorder.

"To the matter at hand, we must find a way to discourage the Santos Development … or at least delay until you convince the Board to reconsider." Madam nodded to both men.

"I couldn't agree with you more, Madam. But at the moment, I've few ideas. The situation with the water system which—as has been pointed out to me this afternoon yet again—is dire. And we don't have the money in the coffers to handle it." Yancy pulled at his tie to loosen it then looked at Madam. She smiled and waved her hand indicating he should continue the effort to find comfort.

"I must apologize for censoring your speech regarding the Midnight Crew. It is still my strong opinion to expose their presence to certain individuals on the Council would result in a witch hunt … something we must avoid."

Yancy nodded. "No need to apologize. Triss warned me but I thought the Council represented all the whole community … every constituent."

"Your wife is a perceptive individual." Madam looked him in the eye. "They do not have a seat on the Council."

"Which needs to change."

"So says Dr. Ramhill. Yancy, she provides health care for them. The physicians in this town are also somewhat limited in their perspectives." Madam said.

"I'm aware … though I admit I didn't take much notice until now. I'm embarrassed, but I know I can trust your discretion." Yancy's smile wiped quickly across his face.

"Yancy, you're a good man with a great heart. You'll lead this town to brighter days, I'm certain." Madam glanced at the leather-bound tomes overflowing the wooden bookcases. "I suspect there are town ordinances in those dusty books which will make their phase one activities a bit more difficult … slowing them down."

"Jonas and I will get on it right away! Madam Miriam, you're a genius." Yancy's smile stayed on his face this time.

"Not at all, Mayor. I'm merely bringing to the forefront an idea you would have seen before the day was out." She rose. Both men jumped to their feet. "Thank you for your time. I will be anxious to know your progress."

Jonas helped her into her coat and held the door.

"Jonas, make some more coffee. We need to get through these old regulations before morning."

"Yes, sir." Jonas entered the outer office nearly bumping into Triss. "Oops, sorry, Triss. I didn't hear you come in."

She held out a basket from which wafted the scent of warm bread. "I've brought Italian meats on fresh rolls. It will keep you fortified until you two finish." She left the basket in his hands and took hold of the doorknob to the inner office. Pausing at the threshold, she looked back at Jonas. "I'm certain making the coffee will take twenty minutes … or perhaps a moment more, won't it, Jonas?"

Without waiting for a reply, she shut and locked the door.

Chapter Eleven

Dawson Hughes visits the Mayor

Jonas pushed the damp bangs from his eyes. He poured water into the coffee maker even though his sour stomach, from too much the night before, screamed at him. Three hours sleep and a quick shower in the gym did little to improve his mood.

The office door swung back against the wall, banging into the brass door stop with a clang. Jonas jumped, fumbling to place the coffee pot under the pouring hot water. He turned around, prepared to yell at the intruder.

A dark windbreaker, Santos Development emblazoned on the left breast, strained to cover the large chested man, his forearms stretching the elastic cuffs to tearing.

"Dawson Hughes. I'm here to see the Mayor," the smoke roughened voice demanded.

"Yes, sir, Mr. Hughes. We're expecting you." Jonas stuck out his hand. Hughes looked him up and down. Jonas rubbed his hand on his pants leg. "I'll see if he is available."

Hughes snorted.

"Mr. Mayor?" Jonas burst through the door, far too loud for the early morning hour. "Mr. Hughes is here. From Santos Corporation."

Yancy stood and straightened his tie. "By all means, Jonas. Show the good fellow in."

Jonas stared at his boss.

"Jonas, don't keep him waiting."

"Sir, yes, sir." Jonas backed out and ushered in Hughes.

Hughes stuck out a brawny hand and pumped Yancy's arm soundly. "Pleased to meet you, Mr. Mayor. We'll be seeing each other often over the next several days, I'm sure."

Yancy motioned to a chair. "Jonas, will you please bring coffee? Mr. Hughes, how do you like yours?"

"It's Dawson and black." Hughes stretched out his legs and reared back on the chair. His bicep muscles rippled under the windbreaker and the grey t-shirt pulled tight over a ripped abdomen.

"Well, then. What can I do for you?" Yancy sat back in his oak swivel chair, sucking in his gut and ruing his very few hours in the gym.

"I want my men to get started as soon as possible. Today. We've several surveys to complete before the contract can be finalized. Once it is, we'll start with the water treatment plant. Complete renovation … bring it into the twenty-first century."

Jonas appeared with two mugs.

"Dawson, you've met my executive assistant, Jonas Steinberg. He will assist you with the paperwork we need before your team starts."

Hughes glanced over his shoulder at Jonas who nodded in response. "Paperwork? My impression was the first phase received council approval yesterday."

"It most certainly did. But there are city and county regulations which come into play with any new building project." Yancy grinned his most convincing smile. "You see, the only access to the zoo property is by water so you need to use barges to transport the heavy equipment. We will have to file water permits with time schedules in order to avoid the shipping industry on the river."

"Forgive my impertinence, Mayor, but there's an access road up along the ridge. We have it on our aerial surveillance." Hughes' smile rivaled Captain Hook's crocodile.

"Yes, yes. There most certainly is but the road runs along easements from the large houses—with rather wealthy owners—and there are limited time periods during the day when it may be used." Yancy held up his hand as Hughes drew breath. "And there is a noise ordinance in place requiring heavy vehicles to maintain a ten miles per hour speed limit. Since the distance from the town to the zoo using the thoroughfare is nearly ten miles ... it will take an hour ... each way."

Hughes laughed from deep in his chest. "Not my problem. I lead the survey team. You will have to take it up with the project boss once my job is done. My team will be walking the area or at the most, using the jeeps. Taking soil samples and soundings."

"Fine ... as long as it is between two and five pm." Yancy pulled a form from the papers on his desk. "We require a complete list of all personnel who will be involved in the survey. All soil samples must be logged through the city Geologist's office before being removed for testing."

Color rose on Hughes' neck. "Ridiculous! We have deadlines and it will take full workdays—even overtime—to meet the schedule."

"I regret any inconvenience but the health of the animals in our small zoo is critically important. They have been under strain with the water situation. The charter is very specific regarding outside intrusion." Yancy leaned back in his swivel chair. "If you are able to make alternate arrangement with the zoo director, it will be at her discretion.

Otherwise, you're most welcome to visit the zoo during morning hours … as a tourist."

Yancy pulled open his lap drawer. He shuffled through the contents. "I should have some passes here in my desk. You'll be my guest and not need to pay the entrance fee." He continued shuffling.

Hughes stood. His hands bunched into fists and opened again. Jonas cleared his throat.

Yancy looked up, surprise flashed across his face at the man towering over him. "Mr. Hughes, you seem upset."

"Mr. Mayor, these concerns are petty at best. I'll speak with the City Council Chair and we'll be clear on the access my men will need to do the job. First and foremost, I need the plats as well as the sewer and water systems schematics."

"Certainly. Jonas, will you please see to retrieving those documents?"

Jonas nodded. "Mr. Hughes, I will have them for you in the morning."

Hughes stepped toward Jonas, towering over him. "I expect them by noon. Today." He glared at him. "I'll send a man by." He pivoted on his heel, facing Yancy. "And there'll not be any obstruction to our work. My bosses are not individuals to be toyed with … nor am I." He turned and left the office. The outer door slammed.

Yancy let out a long sigh. "Jonas, I do believe we made the man angry. What say you?"

Jonas laughed. He pulled a large manila file from the bookcase and laid it on Yancy's desk. Opening it, Yancy ran his finger over the file and extracted maps.

"There. I do believe the maps to the subway burned in the fire in the courthouse … oh, twenty years ago, wasn't it, Jonas?"

105

Jonas cleared his throat. He nodded, took the subway maps
and filed them under Fire Insurance.

Chapter Twelve

Nick and Christian explore the cave

Christian grabbed the rope and jumped onto the rickety dock. He snugged up the rowboat. He looked up just in time to catch the heavy rubber waders Nick threw to him. He set the first pair down and snagged the second. Nick picked up the crossbow.

"Don't toss that." Christian shouted. "It's loaded."

Nick stopped in mid swing. Shifting hands, he handed it to Christian. He hoisted a large duffel bag onto the dock.

"Why do you use a crossbow, anyway?" Nick jumped onto the dock and pulled the heavy waders on snugging the shoulder straps tight.

"You know the old advice 'keep your friends close and your enemies closer'?" Christian grinned. "I don't want my enemies so close. I learned the hard way to use a range weapon when at all possible." He pointed to the sword Nick strapped across his back. "You have an eight-foot reach with your sword. I've gone up against creatures who can spit farther."

Nick grimaced. He pulled the large key from his pocket and inserted into the rusty door. He turned the key, the creaking echoing in the stone chamber. He leaned against the door, shoving with his shoulder. The door groaned open just wide enough for him to edge through sideways.

Christian shifted his crossbow and followed him into the gloom. Nick felt for the light switch. A single naked bulb illuminated the concrete bunker.

"Why build a water treatment plant in a remote cove accessible only by boat?" Christian surveyed the weeping grey stone wall suppressing a shiver. "Who does the maintenance anyway?"

"The gargoyles. Arnie says they don't have a good sense of smell. As to the location, my uncle said it was the town founder's folly. Thought it gave the town a mystique if it depended on water travel … like Venice, I suppose." Nick pulled open the next door leading onto a catwalk. He took a step back as the stench rolled over him. Christian covered his nose with his sleeve fighting not to gag.

"What gave you the bright idea to come here?" Christian wiped his eyes with his cuff.

"When I was growing up, there was a story about a cavern being used by a coven. After all, Salem's not too far away." Nick stepped down the slippery walkway, the handrail wobbling each time he touched it. He glanced down at the two large vats beneath him. The paddles turned, stirring the brown sludge. "According to the story, the entrance to the cavern was in this inlet. The town fathers hanged or drowned the witches including the mayor's wife. They didn't get along very well. He claimed she put a spell on him to cause impotence."

"Did she?" Christian asked as he climb down the ladder following Nick to the floor of the plant.

"Well, if she did, it wasn't very effective. He should have been wearing the scarlet A on his chest … or groin."

"I get the point." Christian readjusted the crossbow on his back.

Nick turned the knob on the metal door in the concrete wall. It did not give. "Do you believe in witches?"

"In my homeland, it is a well-accepted fact witches are real. Everything from hedge witches to the broomstick riding kind. I am grateful Miasma is such a lovely skogkatt. If she were black, I'd have a hard time being in the same room. A bit superstitious of me."

"Skogkatt?" Nick backed away from the door, dropped the duffel and set his feet in a fighting stance.

"The term for the Norwegian forest cat, believed to be a mountain-dwelling fairy cat. They are known for the ability to climb anything … including up a sheer rock face."

Nick pivoted on his front foot and planted a side kick just above the doorknob. The door exploded inward slamming into the stone wall behind it. He flipped the light switch, but the tunnel remained dark.

"Nice footwork." Christian reached for the duffel, but Nick beat him to it. Unzipping it, he pulled out a long package wrapped in plastic. The acrid scent of kerosene stung his nose.

"Torches?" Christian peered over Nick's shoulder.

"Yep. The kids around here have tried to find the cavern, but funny things happen to flashlights once you're about fifty yards in. Scary enough to discourage exploration any deeper. I figured the old-fashioned way might give us a better shot." He pulled out a lighter and lit the first brand. Handing it to Christian, the second flared to life. "These should last about two hours." He ducked into the blackness beyond the door.

Christian followed at a distance to avoid the trailing sparks. He ran his hand over the natural rock wall, the pale moss silky under his fingers. The delicate fronds gleamed bright green in the torch light. "Dragon's gold," he muttered.

"What?" Nick stopped and turned around.

"Something from my childhood." He pointed to the glowing emeralds on the wall. "This moss … it glows. My brother took me spelunking when I was eight. We found a cave with this moss. It is lovely. But there must be light here now and then for it to grow." He raised his torch toward the ceiling. A single bulb hung from a wire just beyond the door. "We should change the bulb on the way back. It would be a shame for these beauties to perish in the total dark."

Christian followed Nick farther into the tunnel. "Exactly what do you hope to find?"

"I don't know. It just seemed like a good time to have a look around." Nick flinched as condensate fell from the roof, sputtering in the torch flame. "Looks like a normal cave structure." He ran his hand along the uneven wall. The floor sloped downward. They walked for several minutes, the only sound the flames crackling and the dripping water.

"I realize it was raining very heavily the other night, but the cistern filled too quickly from the inlets. I wonder if there's an underground stream flowing into the cistern, too. If so, it might be diverted by those teeth-bearing carpets. You're sure they don't get up and walk around on dry land?"

"Sherry assured me they are aquatic." Christian stopped and held his torch up toward the roof. Large spider webs hung from side to side. "If this gets any more Indiana Jones, I am turning around." He chuckled. "I really don't like spiders."

"If there are spiders, there has to be a food source. I'd guess there's access to the surface through a crack or chimney." Nick sniffed the air. "It's fresh except … here, hold this for a moment." He walked farther down the tunnel out beyond the light. His footfalls stopped. Christian counted to one hundred.

Nick reappeared in the light so suddenly Christian jumped, dropping one torch. "How come I heard you going into the tunnel but not coming back?"

Nick shrugged. "Smells like sulfur. The smoke from the torches masks it."

"Sulfur? Brimstone?" Christian picked up the fallen torch, relit it, and handed it to Nick. "Supports Sherry's theory."

"And from the sound of water, there's an underground lake. The tunnel must open into a larger chamber not too far ahead."

"Let's have a look." Christian motioned for Nick to lead the way.

A hundred steps farther, ferocious wind howled down the tunnel, knocking both from their feet. The torches guttered, going dark. Warm water, a knee-deep wave, gushed down the tunnel and swirled around them, challenging their balance.

"I'd say someone is home." Christian crouched against the wall, clutching the crossbow. "And we aren't welcome."

Chapter Thirteen

Dawson offers an invitation

"Dr. Ramhill?" Dawson Hughes stood in the office door, his hat in his hand.

"Yes?" Sherry looked up from the invoices on the desk.

"Excuse the interruption. I wish to introduce myself." His muscular build filled the opening from top to bottom and side to side. "May I come in?" His fingers worried at the fabric of his hat.

Smooth, Sherry thought, not the least sympathetic to his humble act. "The mayor informed me you would be dropping in." She gestured to the vacant chair but did not rise.

Hughes perched on the edge. "I want to complete our survey with minimum disruption to your zoo and its animals. My men just need access for the next day or two depending on what we find about the drainage." He looked up at her, wide eyed. "You understand, don't you?"

Sherry didn't smile. "Of course, I understand. Your company is going to take over the area and tear down the zoo."

"Oh, no, ma'am." Hughes leaned forward in the chair, sincerity written on his face. "The developers want to preserve the zoo within the resort complex. It will be a major draw for visitors and promote tourism."

"Do you really believe that, Mr. Hughes?" Sherry templed her fingers and leaning her elbows on the desk.

"Dawson, please, Dr. Ramhill." He smiled a half smile at her, the gesture not reaching his eyes. "All I know is I lead the survey team. The prospectus requires we determine the project's feasibility from a construction standpoint."

She stared at him, maintaining silence. He fidgeted, worrying his hat in his lap. *Ewww, you should get an Oscar for this performance.* She imitated Madam's stony stare.

"Dr. Ramhill, I have the preliminary artist's concepts for the area. What say I take you to dinner and we can discuss this further?"

Sherry quirked an eyebrow at him.

Hughes cleared his throat. "My men will be here tomorrow morning. If you have someone who can guide them to the points on the premises marked on this map." He pulled a folded paper from his breast pocket and held it out to her. "And my offer is still open for dinner." He looked down at his feet. "I travel a lot and eating alone is the loneliest part." He raised his eyes, once again smiling. "I hope you will accept. Just for dinner."

Sherry took the paper and set it on the desk. She looked at the clock. "I have work to do but I might be free by five." She sighed. "There is a little bistro on the waterfront. *Ombragé.* I will meet you there at five thirty." She stood and held out her hand. He shook it firmly and closed the door behind him.

Sherry remained standing. *Why did I agree to this? I know he is lying.* She picked up her cell phone and sent a message to Micah. Looking out the window over the zoo and the river, she waited for him to arrive.

Chapter Fourteen

Sam and Gene visit the zoo after dark

"Okay, I'll keep the zoo director occupied while you take an unescorted look around." Hughes motioned the two men to sit. They each took chairs, their coveralls at odds with the flowered chintz materials in the hotel suite.

"How many probes do you want us to plant?" Sam filled a cup from the coffee pot on the room service trolley.

"Four should do if you can place them equidistant. If they are off by more than ten feet from the pattern, I'd throw in an extra where you can." Hughes held out his cup for a refill.

"And just how long can you keep the floozy away from the zoo?" Gene rubbed his face with a calloused hand.

Hughes raised an eyebrow at him. "Don't underestimate the charming doctor. She's brighter than I would expect for this backwater. She's also new in town which gives us the edge." He drained his coffee cup and rose, signaling an end to the conversation. "I will keep her away as long as necessary … or perhaps as long as I please."

He herded the two men to the door. "No violence unless absolutely necessary. There's only one other employee and he works a second job at a bar in town. I doubt he'll be there." He shook hands with each. "And if necessary, put the body where it won't be found until we're done here."

He closed the door, threw the safety bolt and whistled on his way to the shower.

Micah toured around the lower levels. He checked each water trough and filled the food trays. He threw fresh alfalfa hay into the compounds for the ungulates. He enjoyed their huffs as they munched on the treat. *I told Dr. Ramhill the truth.* He climbed to the higher compounds. *This is not a job. It's my home. I'll do anything to protect it.*

The large cats prowled their rock outcropping and watched him pass by. They settled down to strip the beef haunches he laid out for them. Micah checked the doors to the reptile house before sliding open the outer hatch to the anaconda cage. He dropped three live mice just inside the opening then walked away without closing the hatch.

Next, the wolverine's den. She sat on the branch, her tail hanging over the edge, swinging back and forth. The cat clock with the pendulum tail flashed through his mind. He masked the thought, knowing the comparison would offend her.

Her eyes glistened in the waning light. Micah smiled, his sharp teeth showing. She returned the feral expression. Micah unlocked the padlock on the wire door and removed it from the hasp, hanging it on the wire fence.

Good evening and happy hunting, Gula, he thought.

Good evening to you as well, young rat. Her near purr washed over him. His toes curled in response. Gula ran her long tongue over her front claws.

Micah disappeared down the path toward the subway entrance. When he turned in, she climbed down and sauntered to the gate. Rising on her hind feet, she reached through the fencing and slid the bar. Pushing open the gate, she disappeared into the tall grass lining the walkway.

Gula padded alongside the gravel pathway nearing the back gate. Extending long claws, she climbed up the oak tree and stretched out on the lowest branch. She rested her head on her paws and stared at the sun creeping behind the cliffs across the river. Musty snake scent reached her nostrils. Tracking the smell, she watched the anaconda drag its nineteen-foot length across the pebbled path and into the brush. With a nod, she returned to her meditative state, ears perked for any intrusion.

She didn't have to wait long. As soon as full dark descended, she heard noises at the back gate.

"Sssshhh."

"What do you want? I have to get this lock open and if the chain rattles, I can't help it." Sam whispered.

"Let me hold the chain." Gene hissed.

"The drone data didn't show any humans in the area. The zoo's closed. The director is having dinner with the boss and the helper is gone." Sam continued prying at the rusted lock. "Some security."

"Probably never needed any." Gene scanned the bushes, fidgeting with the probe in his hand.

"Remember those teenagers who broke into a zoo in Buffalo a few years ago? One fell into the polar bear compound and was ripped limb from limb." Sam pulled the hasp off the chain and fed the chain through the gate. He pushed it open.

"Pleasant thought. Let's just stay away from the polar bears, why don't we?" Gene eased through the opening and swung the gate closed. He fed the chain back through and tucked the lock into place, leaving it unlocked.

"Worried about the constabulary in this two-bit town?" Sam jabbed him with an elbow. "From the potholes in the road, they don't make regular rounds up this way."

116

"Okay, okay. Just being careful." Gene settled the night goggles over his eyes and flipped the switch. "Where do we start?"

Sam adjusted his own goggles and surveyed the walkway. "Go about thirty feet north and I'll go this way. Meet back here."

Gene walked under the branch, Gula's dangling tail grazing his neck. He swatted at it. She held back a growl but flicked her tail catching him in the ear. He swung around, looking in all directions except up.

"Damn moths," he mumbled. Counting his paces to measure out thirty feet, he pulled a small trowel from his utility belt and dug into the muddy earth. He felt in his pocket for the probe and dropped the golf ball sized unit into the hole.

Brush rattled near his leg. Gene startled, peering in the dim light. He cringed backward, his mouth going dry, as the large snake slithered across his foot and stuck its wedge-shaped head into the newly dug hole. Jumping back, he tripped over a coil and fell flat on his rear. The snake twisted to look at him as it closed its mouth over the probe. Gene crab-walked backwards, scooting over two more writhing coils. He pushed one coil off his leg feeling it tightening, then stood and ran in the direction Sam had gone.

"Sam, Sam" he hissed in the darkness. Sam stepped from the bushes and tapped Gene on the shoulder. Gene jumped, screaming.

"Shhh." Sam punched him in the shoulder. "What's wrong with you?"

"Snake bi bi big snake." Gene pulled off his goggles and wiped his face with his bandana. "Nearly ate my foot."

Sam punched him in the arm again. "What about the temple in Honduras? There were snakes everywhere."

117

"Yeah, but they were little snakes. This one could eat an elephant." Gene stepped away from Sam. "And don't punch me again!"

"Okay, but did you get the probe in the ground?" Sam tamped down the disturbed earth with his foot.

"No."

"Why not?" Sam pulled off his goggles and wiped the lenses with his shirt tail.

"Snake ate it."

"You're kidding me."

"Nope. Grabbed it up in its mouth. Swallowed it. Must have thought it was an egg."

Sam sighed. "I've got one down and an extra in my pocket. We'll just shift the square. If we can get three more in the right places, it'll be enough. Let's get to the next sites. Down this way." Sam led off.

"Hope the damn snake gets indigestion," Gene muttered.

The two men walked down the pathway between the compounds for the carnivores and rounded the corner to enter the central courtyard. Sam pulled the map from his pocket along with a small flashlight. "We need to get into the lower area. The path should be over there." He pointed to an opening between tall hedges.

Entering the path, Gene stopped and grabbed Sam by the shoulder.

"What now?" Sam demanded.

"There's something in the bushes over there." Gene pointed to a spot several feet ahead. "I heard it rustle."

"I doubt the snake could move fast enough to get ahead of us." Sam shrugged off Gene's hand. "Come on. You're starting to give me the heebie jeebies." He set off at a trot.

118

Gene followed close behind, stumbling as he tried to keep an eye on the underbrush. He ran into Sam, knocking him off his feet and into the bushes.

"Damn it, Gene. Get your wits about you." Sam took the offered hand. "It's a zoo. They attract different birds, squirrels—"

"But it's nighttime. Those things don't come out at night." Gene shook his head while scanning the bushes.

"Maybe not but opossums and skunks do." Sam grabbed him by the shoulders and shook him. "Get a grip. Let's get these last ones planted and get out."

Gene nodded.

Sam's tone softened as he patted his friend's back. "I heard there's a good bar in town. Stays open extra late. I'll buy the first round."

Gene smiled weakly. "Okay. Where to?"

Sam pointed to the right-hand walkway. "Down the way about twenty feet should do it." He headed off in the opposite direction, looking around at every shaking leaf. *He's got me seeing things, too. Man, this is the weirdest night and that's saying a lot given what we've been through with the boss.* He stopped counting his steps and reached down to dig the hole for the probe.

A paw landed on his hand, caging it with long black claws. Sam froze staring at the razor-sharp points. He held his breath. His hand shaking, he dropped the probe from his free hand. A second paw scooped the probe from his other hand, rolling it into the underbrush. The paw patted his captured hand twice then withdrew into the darkness under the bushes.

Sam's mind raced inside his petrified body, his heart pounding. He stared at the spot where the paw disappeared unable to decide whether to run or faint. The leaves rustling

119

decided for him and he backed away stumbling on the loose stones.

Two dark eyes glinted in the moonlight. A snout filled with white teeth as long as his fingers emerged from the shadows. Sam fled up the walkway, barely feeling the ground.

Stupid, stupid, stupid. Never run from an animal. Stupid, ran through his mind but he failed to stop his feet.

Gula loped along behind him. She chuckled then let out a ferocious growl. Sam ran faster.

"Gene, Gene, Gene. To the gate." Sam reached the gate, fumbled with the chain, his hands wet and trembling. After three attempts, he pulled the chain loose, swung the gate open and dove through. He hung onto the edge to swing it shut behind him. Gula stopped a few yards from the gate and dropped into a sitting position, her lips pulled back in a sneer.

Gene appeared from the darkness, skidding to a halt when he saw Gula. "What the hell?"

Gula turned her dark gaze on him. Gene's face lost all color.

"Just stay calm," Sam whispered.

"Easy for you to say. You're out there." Gene gulped.

"It didn't attack me." Sam edged the gate open a few inches. "Just walk very slowly to the gate."

Gene measured the distance between the gate and Gula. He stepped sideways, cringing. Gula licked one paw, worrying her claws. Gene took another step. Gula looked over at him. She yawned showing all the cutting teeth.

Gene took two steps ... then another. He reached out one hand, his fingers brushing the metal gate. Gula rose up on her hind legs and snarled at him. Sam swung the gate open and Gene scrambled through. Sam slammed the gate shut and fumbled for the lock.

Gula ambled over to the gate and placed both front paws on the grating. She stood mid chest high. Sam reached once more for the lock. Gula nibbled his fingers, chortling. He drew back slowly, grasping the padlock and fed it through the latch, keeping his fingers as far away as possible.

Gula dropped back onto all fours then sat on her haunches. She glared at the men running for their jeep. The anaconda edged his head under Gula's front leg.

"Good night's work, I'd say" Miasma sauntered from the shadows. She head-butted Gula.

The anaconda belched.

Chapter Fifteen

Sherry learns a lesson then has coffee at the Bar

In the bright morning sun, Sherry strolled down the path through Madam's garden on her way to the zoo. Petri buzzed by her ear. She held up a hand for him to alight. He wobbled as he landed, a large purple Hyacinth over his shoulder. He bowed, nearly overbalancing and offered it to Sherry. She grabbed it as he back stepped and toppled off her palm.

"Petri, this is lovely. Thank you."

Fluttering back to his perch on her palm, the small pixie bowed again with more grace, then stuck out his hand.

Sherry considered this situation for a moment. She inspected his hand. *No buzzer or other tricky device.* "Let's see. Hyacinth is a bloom in the language of flowers. While I didn't appreciate the hours spent with a book on my head for posture, I did enjoy the medieval idea flower bouquets could send a message. White Hyacinth, as I recall, stands for loveliness … which would be a charming compliment."

Petri shook his head.

"So, you don't find me lovely?" Sherry chuckled at the distress on the pixie's face. "I am just teasing, Petri." She hurried on before he could worry more. "Blue means constancy. And I know your first love is Madam."

Petri blushed.

"Purple … purple." Sherry's brow knit in concentration. "Of course, sorrow … meaning 'Please forgive me.'" She held out her little finger toward Petri. "I forgive you. Shake on our friendship." Petri grabbed her finger in both hands and shook it up and down. He jumped in the air and disappeared into the camellias.

"This is a good start to the morning." She found the hidden gate and entered the zoo. The door to the wolverine den stood ajar. Brow wrinkling, she scanned the area for her. Bright eyes watched from the limb. The wolverine raised a paw as if in greeting and then returned to her morning nap.

She found the padlock hanging open on the wire mesh beside the door. *How odd. Perhaps Mica knows something about this.* She snapped it shut and continued toward her office. Along the way, she found long sinuous track marks in the pebble walkway, suggesting an object dragged through the stones. *Odder still.* She veered away from her original destination toward the elephant compound. Every morning at this time, Micah watered the elephants. *And gives them a good shower.* She smiled, their play having amused her on days past.

The juvenile male elephant gamboled in the water puddle. Micah held the hose, sending the water in an arc across the female elephant's back. Sherry paused to watch the fun. In a few moments, Micah turned to wave at her, the hose spraying across the distance and Sherry ducked back from the droplets falling in her direction. Micah froze until Sherry laughed aloud and waved back at him. He bent to turn off the water at the faucet. The young elephant lumbered forward and whacked Micah across the backside with his trunk. Micah fell face down in the mud.

Sherry bit her tongue to control her laughter, not wanting to embarrass him. The elephant grabbed Micah's belt and lifted him into the air. Micah struggled to get his feet on the ground. Once righted, he swept around and wrapped both arms around the gray head. Ears flapping, the trunk returned the hug to Micah's waist. Finally released, Micah approached Sherry, scraping mud from his clothes.

He stopped a few feet from her. "Good morning, Dr. Ramhill."

"It appears you have had a fine morning yourself, Micah." Sherry's cheeks hurt trying not to smile.

"All in good fun but I'd best find dry clothes." Micah headed for the employee locker room with Sherry at his shoulder.

"Micah, I came in the back entrance and I noticed the wolverine compound was not locked. Can you tell me anything about it?"

"I must have missed it when I closed up last night." Micah kept his eyes averted. "But there were—"

Sherry stopped him with a hand on his arm. "Micah, her cage needs to stay locked at all times. Wolverines are extraordinarily dangerous." She said, her face stern.

"Gula." Micah said, his eyes flashing.

"I know her species, Micah. It is *Gulo gulo* which is Latin for glutton." Sherry slipped into her lecturing mode.

"She is not a glutton!" Micah stepped close to her, his face red. "She's a very lean and lithe lady. And her name is Gula—with an 'a'."

Sherry stared at him. "Oh."

"Dr. Ramhill, all the animals here have names—not just the wolverine or the …" he stuttered. "The elephant who knocked me in the mud is Badal. He's an Asian Elephant and he was born during a very heavy rain. His mother is Mahika."

"Badal means clouds or monsoon." Sherry said almost in a whisper. Micah stood looking at her, his hands bunched in his pockets. "And Mahika means dew drops. Micah, I

124

apologize. I have been too distracted and too thick pated to take the time to get to know —really get to know—the animals. I am truly sorry."

Micah nodded, his shoulders relaxing.

"But Gula can't be let loose in the zoo." Sherry's tone turned firm.

"Dr. Ramhill, I tried to tell you there were two men in the zoo last night. Gula and Cuddles chased them out."

"Who were they?" Sherry's voice raised. "What did they want?

"They were planting these in the ground." He held out an egg-shaped sensor. She lifted it with two fingers from his muddy palm. She sank down on the bench outside the office.

Turning the probe over in her hand, she motioned for Micah to sit. "Where did you find this?"

"Gula gave it to me. She took it from them. She said he was tall and thin with reddish brown hair. The other one was shorter and heavy set." He paused. "And balding. She thinks Cuddles may have caused more hair loss."

"Cuddles, I deduce, is the anaconda."

Micah nodded, a smile lighting his face. "You're catching on."

Sherry returned the smile then her brow wrinkled. "A man from the Santos Development is due this morning to take some measurements. We need to keep a close eye on him and perhaps throw up a few hurdles in his path." She winked at Micah. "And see if he fits the description."

Micah stood, offering his muddy hand to help her up. "Your wish is my command, my lady."

She looked at his dirty fingers then took the hand and stood. She squeezed it before letting go and resisted the urge to wipe it on her skirt. Her cell phone rang.

"Hello?"

"Dr. Ramhill, this is Anastasia. You had a call from Nick. He would like you to join him at the bar as soon as possible." Anastasia clicked off the call.

"Interesting." Sherry pulled the SUV keys from her purse. "Micah, you are in charge … as usual. Do anything you can to disrupt the gentleman's work without being too obvious."

"Yes, ma'am."

"And be careful."

"Ma'am?"

"There's more here than we yet know."

"Yes, ma'am."

Sherry headed for the delivery gate where the Zoo SUV stood in the early morning sun.

***

"When do we take another look?" Sherry sipped on her coffee, her elegant legs crossed, the shapely calf drawing all eyes. Christian started at her voice, drawing a smile from her.

"Emmm. I don't know." He shrugged and looked at Nick.

"We?" Nick looked over the rim of his mug.

Sherry leaned forward elbows on the table, her nose as close to Nick as she could stretch. "Yes, we. I am in this up to my pretty little neck, too, you know."

Nick stared at her, his dark eyes black in the shadows. "We …" he stressed the word, "don't have any idea what is down there. It will mostly likely be very dangerous."

Sherry sneered at him.

126

"Whatever it is, it orchestrated our dunking—and I add—near drowning in the cistern. If not for Christian's bolt." He paused.

"We would have gotten out through the manhole cover at the top." Sherry finished for him.

Gino set the coffee pot on the table and bowed his way back to the bar. He lifted two margarita glasses letting loose the chastised pixies. "Shhhh." he warned. "The Boss isn't in a good mood so shoo." Both pixies disappeared with an "eeep".

Sherry caught Gino's eye, her sides shaking. Gino's lip twitched and he busied himself wiping the bar.

"Dr. Ramhill," Nick leaned forward until they were nose to nose. "You are not going with us."

Sherry sat up straight. "I most certainly am, or I will find someone who will take me." She looked around the bar. "Like Arnie or … or … or Gregariel."

"Both are smart enough to say no." Nick glared at her.

"Oh, you think so? We will just see." She scooted her chair back.

Christian grabbed her hand, turning it palm up and running his finger along her lifeline. A thrill ran down Sherry's spine. "I see here several small interruptions. Do you really want to make one permanent?"

She pulled at her hand, but Christian tightened his grip. Sherry gave up without much effort. Christian continued tracing the line.

"I certainly do not." She pointed a finger at her heart line. "But observe this one. It is strong and deep as for all the Ramhills. It is known as the dragon heart line. No coercion will dissuade me from seeking the very chamber you describe." She looked each in the eye.

Nick reared back on his chair. "What would Madam Miriam say?"

Sherry jerked her hand from Christian's hold. Her back ramrod straight, a stance which would make Madam proud, she glared down at him. "I will not discuss this further. Madam Miriam does not tell me what to do."

Nick chuckled under his breath. Sherry pivoted on her perfect three-inch heel and swept the chair legs out from under him, sending him backwards. The crack as his head contacted the floor echoed in the silent bar. He shook his head and attempted to rise but fell back with the same heel pressing down on his chest.

Sherry leaned to glare at him. "I am going with you. Do you understand me?"

Nick nodded, his eyes rolling.

"Very good. I will be back in an hour."

He lay still listening to her heels click up the stairs to the street.

Christian slipped his hands under Nick's shoulders and hoisted him to his feet. An ice pack settled on his neck.

"That went rather well, don't you think?" Christian laughed from behind him. Nick elbowed him in the gut.

Chapter Sixteen

Dawson gives Sam and Gene their marching orders

"What the hell do you mean, the snake ate it?" Dawson tipped the breakfast table over and grabbed Gene by the shirt front, pulling him up onto his toes.

"Boss, just what I said. It was a big snake. It snatched the probe from the hole and swallowed it." Gene gripped Dawson's mitt-sized hands, wheezing for breath.

Dawson dropped him. "So, you ran?"

Sweat beaded on Gene's nose. "No, sir. I just backed away."

Dawson snarled at Sam. Sam picked up a cup and poured coffee, the cup shaking visibly.

"Sam?" Dawson allowed Gene to escape. Gene crouched behind the easy chair in the corner.

"Sir?" Sam took another sip.

"What happened next?" Dawson took the cup from Sam's hand.

"Then the wolverine took the next one." Sam reached for the cup.

Dawson threw it against the wall. "What are you two smoking? A wolverine? Have you lost your mind? If there was a wolverine in this mess, you'd both be shreds too small to sweep up."

Sam squared his shoulders. "It's exactly what it was, sir. It took the probe from my hand and chased us to the gate." He tried to look away from Dawson's scrutiny. "She was laughing at us. I swear it."

Dawson filled his lungs, his chest muscles straining his oxford shirt. He exhaled and inhaled again, his hands itching for Sam's neck. "Sam, if you weren't the best electronics man I have, I'd be tossing you out the window. You might hit the river from here." Dawson stalked to the window and stared at the muddy water. Tangled limbs floated swiftly by, a soggy box trapped in its midst.

Sam motioned Gene to stand up and get out from behind the chair. Gene shook his head. Dawson turned from the window. He stared at each man before he spoke.

"Sam, you're going to the zoo this morning and you're going to get those readings. I already convinced the lovely director you'd would be there today to take measurements. They'll be expecting you."

Sam nodded. "What about Gene?"

"He'll be busy surveying the sewer and the drainage system." He set the table back on its feet and motioned to Gene. Grabbing up his briefcase, he found the city map. "The idiots in City Hall insist the schematic was destroyed in a fire. But, there's an entrance to the storm drain system right here on the old subway map." He snorted. "Imagine. A subway in this backwater. I doubt it ever worked." He pointed to the black circle. "Start there and find the way toward the zoo. I want to know every inch. We need to find if there is an access to the area where the artifact appears to be."

Gene peered at the diagram committing it to memory.

"Take Eric with you. He can keep a level head." Dawson stared into Gene's eyes until he flinched. "He'll scare away the booglies."

Sam and Gene ran for the door. Dawson's derisive laughter chased them down the hallway.

Chapter Seventeen

Sherry visits Professor Lizzard with two dozen

Sherry steered the white SUV up the steep road to the observatory. Parking under the overhanging walkway, she climbed the two flights to the door and knocked. The metal door vibrated with a deep bell tone.

"What? What? Who's there?" The voice came from above. Sherry backed away from the door, clutching the railing as she leaned out into space and looking upward.

"Professor Lizzard, Sherry again." The wind carried her voice away, blowing her long hair into her face. The Professor peered over from the balcony above. The sun behind him hid his face in shadow.

"Well, inopportune as the time may be, have you brought more cookies?" Lizzard's plea brought a smile from her.

"Of course, sir. It would be terribly rude not to bring refreshments. After all, it is nearly elevenses and I would guess you haven't stopped for lunch."

Vincent held out his gaunt arm and peered at an oversized watch dangling on his wrist. "How astute, my dear. The door is not locked. Do come in and join me in the upper chamber." His dark form disappeared.

Sherry juggled the two cookie boxes and pushed open the heavy door. The first flight led to the chamber she visited before and it took a few moments to discover the second flight hidden behind an ornamental metal screen.

She worked her way up the spiral grated stairway. *Glad I changed into boots.* As she achieved the landing, long warm fingers lifted the boxes from her. The other hand slid under her elbow and guided her to a seat.

"Forgive the darkened room." His voice sounded close to her then moved away into the gloom. "I'm taking measurements which are rather light sensitive."

Muffled crunching reached her ears. "That is quite fine, Professor. I see rather well in the dimness. Another family trait."

His fingers wrapped around her hand and nestled a warm cup in her palm.

"Thank you."

"Cookie?"

She reached into the box he held. Her fingers found one lonely cookie remaining from the two dozen originally nestled within. "Thank you, again."

"I was meaning to call upon you at the zoo. Nigel and I've come up with some interesting theories regarding the presence in the waterways." Lizzard sat on a low bench across from her.

"And I have news for you from Nick and Christian." Sherry's eyes grew more accustomed to the low light. Professor Lizzard's broad grin appeared then she could make out his eyes. *I wonder if Miasma taught him her trick?*

"By all means, give it a go, young lady." Lizzard leaned back on the bench and crossed his arms.

Sherry caught the suggestion of his shadow tail balancing him. Recounting the adventure at the water treatment plant, she added her own evaluation. "I think whatever brought the entity here disrupts anything electrical … like batteries in the flashlights." She took a deep breath. "The bolt from

133

Christian's crossbow hurt it sufficiently that it let down the subterfuge we were walled in. It must have used its body to block the waterway." She paused, her brow furrowed. "It must be very strong to hold back the water."

"Strong or magical." Lizzard interjected.

"Your turn, Professor. What have you and my illustrious uncle discovered?"

Lizzard templed his long spatulated fingers and rocked on his tail. "From the analysis, we have determined the Sulphur content mixed with other rare minerals suggests it's from Hell's third level."

"Are you suggesting a demon?" Sherry bit her lip.

"Certainly, who else would be carrying brimstone?" Lizzard's eye sockets swiveled to stare at her. "And the attraction has something to do with the peculiar leylines."

"What peculiarity?" Sherry took a deep breath, trying to regain color in her face.

"Something is feeding energy into the leylines—starting in the caves beyond the zoo and emanating outward along the minor lines." Lizzard rose. "Here, my dear," he held out his hand. "Let's look at the map and I will show you the readings."

Sherry laid her hand in his large palm. The fingers closed around her own and lifted her from her seat. As she stepped around the bench, she scooted the two empty cookie boxes under the bench with her foot.

She shook her head, wishing she'd snuck a cookie in the car.

Professor Lizzard switched on a small light under the long work table and the map spread across its surface glowed from beneath. Sherry studied the expected landmarks and markings which were overlaid with a spider web of gold lines, some darker than others. The lines emanated outward from a point just to the north of the zoo. She traced the lines with her elegant fingernail. She noticed the Professor following her fingertip.

"Professor, is this a nexus?"

Lizzard startled from his reverie. "Do you and Mim—er—Madam Miriam have the same manicurist?"

Sherry turned her palm outward, pointing her fingers upward. "Why, yes. She recommended a lovely lady in town—though she does keep only evening hours and works in very dim light. But she does a wonderful job." She held her hand out to admire the rich color. "Why do you ask?"

Lizzard's complexion paled. "No reason ... except for the excellent work." He cleared his throat. "Yes, you are perceptive. This is a nexus, and, as you can see, it is in proximity to the zoo. Unfortunately, where there should be a great outpouring, there is only a trickle." He extracted a long yellow sheet and handed it to her. "Here are the actual readings. Interestingly, they fluctuate ... weaker during the day and stronger at night."

Sherry scanned the numbers and finally shook her head. She handed the page back to Lizzard. "I confess, Professor, the measurements hold little meaning for me."

"Your uncle and I also scratched our heads over it until he found similar sites in Europe with which to compare." He straightened his back, cracking echoing through the observatory dome. "There are three known sites in England, France and Spain where nexi occur with readings this weak. They are all areas in which the Merlins have been absent for more than three or four hundred years."

"Professor, who is balancing the leylines?"

"There was rumor years ago a device developed by a steampunk Merlin would run automatically. Nigel believes

135

such a device is possible but there are no records it was ever developed ... or if it was successful." Professor Lizzard licked his lips, searching for the cookie boxes. Spying one under the table, he retrieved it faster than Sherry could track his movements. He held the box over his head and caught the last crumbs on his tongue. "Hmmmm. Those were very good."

Sherry fought the urge to laugh at his wistful expression. "Professor, I will bring more next time I come." She patted his hand.

"Will you? You are a dear one." Professor Lizzard pecked her on the cheek. "And the answer to the next question is yes. Nigel is adamant if such a device exists, there may well be one here and the weak reading suggest it is in need of repair."

Sherry stared at the spot on the map. "Do you believe there is a tunnel from the water treatment plant to a cave or cavern right around here?" She pointed at the intersection.

Professor Lizzard pulled another map from the bookshelf. "These are measurements by three-dimensional underground laser scanners. They are such fun to use!" His eyes danced, the nictitating membrane fluttering. "If I overlay the topographic map, you can see where there are open spaces all along the river bank. See here?" He pointed to an area to the south. "These are the tunnels dug for the trolley. Some are natural and others were dug out to run across town." He paused. "And these are Madrecita's doing ... the safe areas for her clan."

Sherry focused on the area beneath the zoo. "This must be the catch basin we were in." She followed a small winding tunnel to the north. "It is connected to this large open area" She leaned closer to read the distance chart. "About half a mile from the water treatment plant."

She stood and held out her hand to Professor Lizzard. "Sir, you have given me what I need to know. Thank you."

"Young lady, do promise to come back and tell me your discoveries." He deposited the empty cookie box in the waste receptacle and sighed.

"I most certainly will." Her boot heels clicked down the metal steps. She pushed on the outer door securing it against the rising wind.

"Dr. Ramhill," Lizzard's voice sounded above her.

She looked up at him on the catwalk.

"Don't forget there could be a demon."

Sherry shuddered.

Chapter Eighteen

Sam meets Garnet

"Whatcha' doin'?"

The voice materialized at his elbow and Sam jumped, dropping the probe into the hole.

"Damn!" He turned looking for the voice. "Where are you, you little rat?"

"Up here." A strawberry blonde girl jumped from the limb, landing near Sam's feet. She grabbed his leg to swing around him and peered down the hole. "Whatcha' drop?" Before he could answer, she dove into the hole coming up with the probe in her hand. "What's this do?"

Sam snatched the probe from her long fingers and blew the dirt from the sensitive membrane. Large brown eyes stared up at him. "Uh, thanks, kid. Now get lost."

"Oh, I can't get lost. I know this zoo like the back of my hand." She held her tiny fist out. "Funny, I think this one's mine."

Sam caught himself before he laughed. He didn't have time to be distracted. The boss wanted answers by tonight and half the day was gone. *Damn zoo. Why did it have to be near a zoo? Her assistant cost me the whole morning, moving animals from one place to another.*

"Don't talk much, do you, mister?" Sam jumped again as the voice came from directly behind him.

"Stop that." Sam shouted

"Stop what?"

"Startling me." Sam turned to look at her.

"You goin' to drop the thingy again?" Garnet squinted at the device in his hand. "What's it do?"

"You asked me already." Sam pulled the wires from his tool box and attached the probe to the meter.

"And you didn't answer." She spun around him, kneeling down by the meter. "So, I asked again." She poked a finger at the dial.

Sam slapped her hand away. "This device is very sensitive so don't touch."

Garnet sucked on her fingers, tears welling in her eyes.

"Ah, don't cry. I didn't slap you that hard." Sam squatted down to eye level. "Look, I have a job to do and you're distracting me. I have to be done before it gets dark. So why don't you run along?" She blinked back the tears, long eyelashes glistening with moisture. "Please?"

Garnet took two steps toward the fence around the compound. She stopped. "But you didn't answer my question." She stuck out her lower lip and firmed up her stance.

Sam sighed. "It's a listening device. It tells me what's under the ground. Things like underground rivers and caves."

"Caves don't make any noise, silly."

He smiled at her. "Do you know how bats find things in the dark?"

She nodded, screwing up her mouth. "Sure, with sound waves."

"This device does much the same thing. I send a sound wave through the ground, and, when the echo comes back, I can tell if the ground is solid or if there is a hollow space." He looked up at the darkening sky. "Now, I've answered your question. Please let me finish my work." He picked up the earphones.

"Can I try?" Garnet moved forward.

"No!" Sam held them beyond her reach. "Hey, I think I hear your mother calling you."

"No, you don't." Garnet bounced from one foot to the other. "If she were calling me, you'd hear her voice right beside you."

"What?"

"She's a ventriloquist. She can throw her voice anywhere … even out here." Garnet turned to look at the gate. "Oh, I remember. Dr. Sherry said she was going to move Billy Boy to this pasture for better grazing. I'd better go." She disappeared into the bushes.

Sam heaved a heavier sigh and turned back to the meter. *Billy Boy?* His head snapped up. The bison bull amble toward him. He slowly tucked the earphones in his bag, picked up the meter and backed toward the fence. Billy Boy followed him, ears perked and huffing.

When Sam felt the fence at his back, he threw his gear over and scaled the fence. Billy Boy snorted at him through the metal uprights. Miasma perched on Billy Boy's hump, her sides shaking with laughter. She patted Billy Boy on his massive head.

Sam ran for his truck.

Chapter Nineteen

Three return to the cave

Christian admired Sherry's lithe figure. Even though she was dressed in a camouflage jumpsuit, it hugged her body in all the right places. He adjusted the quarter staff on his back and picked up his crossbow.

Nick punched him on the arm. They passed through the antechamber to the sewage treatment plant. "Ready?" he inquired.

"Not really but what the hell."

Sherry pulled a small pistol from her pocket. She popped the clip then inserted it back into the pistol with a click. Nick raised an eyebrow.

"Don't worry, I know how to use this." From her opposite pocket, she pulled a similar device. "This one's a tranquilizer. It will take down an elephant in twenty steps." She saw their smiles. "I know, it may be too late if we are talking demon here, but it is better than nothing."

"Demon?" Christian's puzzled look made Sherry smile.

"Oh, didn't I mention it?" She studied her fingernails, not meeting their eyes. "Professor Lizzard is fairly certain the brimstone indicates a demon may be involved here. What better place for one than an underground cavern?" She smiled brightly at the two, their grim faces chilling her.

"And you were going to tell us this when?" Nick clenched the sword in his hand.

"I just did." Sherry carefully tucked the tranquilizer gun back into her pocket and straightened her jump suit, settling the broad belt around her waist.

Nick stepped toward her, forcing her to look up at him. "Listen, I don't like the fact you're along, and I don't like the fact we aren't certain what we are facing down there. But," He placed his finger under her chin and tipped her head farther back, his breath warm on her face. "You will do exactly as Christian or I tell you, and you won't stop to argue. Do I make myself clear?"

Sherry stepped back, bumping into Christian. He held her arms to steady her with a little more pressure than she thought necessary. "What if you tell me one thing and he tells me another?" She squirmed in his grip.

Nick growled and pushed open the door to the sewage plant. The noisome vapors engulfed her. She gulped, grinned and tried to breathe through her mouth.

Gads, that's supposed to work. Now I taste it, too! She gulped again, fighting her stomach. Christian released her, and she staggered into Nick. He stopped in the doorway, standing still until she stood on her own.

She followed him across the catwalk carefully looking away from the swirling vats below. A strong hand engulfed her fingers and wrist assisting her down the rusted iron stairs. At the bottom, Nick opened the door to the tunnel. He dropped the duffel bag and handed a torch to each.

While Nick used his lighter on the torch in Sherry's hand, Christian muttered and touched his own with a fingertip. The flame flared up glinting off the sword in Nick's hand. The runes on the blade flared in the light varying from green to red. Christian shook his head, his face ashen in the eerie dance. Nick and Sherry stared at him. He mumbled something about dropping his match and scuffed at the floor with his boot.

142

Sherry gulped in the fresher air from the tunnel, grateful her stomach now objected to the butterflies in it rather than the stench. She held the torch up high to peer into the tunnel. "How old is this?"

Nick paused. "The treatment plant is nearly one hundred years old … with upgrades through the years. The tunnel is a natural formation so who knows?"

His voice echoed in the narrow corridor. He held a finger to his lips. Leaning close to Sherry, he whispered, "We'd best keep voices down. The less we alert the inhabitant, the better."

Sherry chuckled inwardly. *As if we haven't already.* She nodded agreement.

The three set off at a quick pace, stepping lightly on the shard littered floor. The air grew colder as they twisted around small stalagmites. Nick held up his hand. Sherry and Christian drew close.

"This is as far as we got last time. Stay close." He edged farther into the tunnel. Standing still, Sherry marveled at the silence of Nick's footsteps. *Actually, no sound at all. Does he levitate?* Christian nudged her from behind.

Around a sharp corner, the tunnel opened into a large cavern, the light from the flames barely illuminating the next few steps. The sound of bubbling water echoed against the granite walls.

"Hot springs?" Sherry whispered. Her question went unanswered.

Nick sidestepped to the right, his back against the cavern wall. The others followed. A few yards farther, the light reflected off the water. White foam played across the surface and steam rose in languid tentacles toward the ceiling. He motioned for them to go back. Retracing their steps, they continued to the left. They found a firmer path. A tall stalagmite nearly filled the path.

Nick handed Sherry his torch and stretched his arms around the stalagmite. The edge narrowed to room for toes only. He inched his way forward until he disappeared from view. His hand reached back around Sherry assumed for the torch. She leaned as far as she could to hand it to him, overbalanced, heading nose first for the water.

Christian grabbed her belt, hauling her back onto solid ground. Nick snatched the torch from midair. As the light played across the surface, a woolly body lurched up, whirling teeth grazing Nick's hand. He pulled back slamming against the wall. The *teppich* smacked onto the cavern floor, squirming after him. He pulled his sword and smacked the creature across the head with the flat of the blade.

"Don't hurt it!" The deep rumbling deafened Nick. He cringed but continued pushing the *teppich* back into the water.

"I said ..." Louder and more insistent, the voice drew closer. "Don't hurt it." The echoes played again and again in the stone space.

"I didn't ... except for a headache." Nick held the torch above his head trying to locate the speaker.

"Nick, a little help here!" Christian called for Nick's attention. Sherry's hand waved from around the stalactite. Nick grabbed her by the wrist, swinging her out over the water. He pulled her sharply back to him. She banged into his chest, the breath knocked from her. She bent over gasping. He pounded her on the back once ... twice. Then moved her aside as Christian edged his way to the wider ledge.

Pushing Sherry against the wall, Christian stepped beside Nick. "Any ideas?"

144

"Ten yards ahead, the ledge widens out." Nick raised the torch a little higher and strained against the inky darkness. "Whatever it is, It's either up on the wall or a lot taller than us."

"Remember, it could be a demon," Sherry hissed from behind them. She pushed between them, sniffing at the air. "The air is moving. It is fresh though you can still smell a little brimstone."

Nick chuckled as Christian followed Sherry's example.

"Definitely. I would say it's coming from our right." Christian handed Sherry his torch then pulled a small wool ball from his pouch. He stuck the quarrel through it. It burst into flames. He fired into the unseen heights. The arrow arced upward, falling into the darkness.

"There." Sherry pointed to a position twenty feet above them along the back wall. "Eyes, I definitely saw eyes. Big eyes."

Christian nocked a second quarrel and aimed. The arrow sailed into the darkness then a large grey-green scaled claw swatted it from the air. It clattered to the stone floor.

"Ouch." Boredom dripped from the word.

"May we talk about this situation?" Sherry yelled.

"No." The word reverberated through the cave.

A claw grabbed Nick from the ledge, flinging him into the water. The surface boiled with the agitated *teppich*. Nick's head broke the surface and he scrambled to the pool's edge, kicking back at the *teppich* chewing on his boot. He scrabbled at the ledge. A second *teppich* leapt onto his back.

Christian pushed Sherry against the wall again, ignoring her irritated glare. He charged the large reptilian body, his quarterstaff held as a lance. The long sinewy tail swept his feet from under him, knocking him down face first. A claw shot out and snatched the quarterstaff from midair. The demon snapped the staff in half, dropping the pieces on Christian's back.

Nick shook himself, reaching for the *teppich* on his back. It held on tight to his belt. Sherry shoved her fist against the corner of jaw, prying open its teeth. It rolled back into the water.

"Sorry," she whispered to the *teppich*.

Rocks in the walls glowed, dimly at first but increasing until the cavern was fully illuminated. Light reflected off the turbulent water filled with many more creatures.

Nick pulled his sword. He moved toward Christian giving him cover to rise. They stood shoulder to shoulder for a moment, then moved apart to place the demon between them. It sat on a ledge fifteen feet above the floor, its tail draped to the floor.

"Round two?" it inquired.

Before they could respond, it descended on giant wings landing upon them. One claw wrapped around Christian and pinned him to the ground. A hind foot caught Nick in the chest, his sword making no indent in the scaly hide. The demon sat down … on him.

Sherry stepped forward. She curtseyed to the demon showing empty hands and rising before her knocking knees landed her on the floor. "It is most kind to provide light for us." She waved her hand at the glowing wall. "We do have limited ability in the dark."

"I'd say you have limited ability in the light as well." The demon tightened her grip on Christian eliciting a groan echoed by Nick as she shifted her weight, her heavy thigh across his back.

"You are correct." She paused considering her approach. Her heart beat in her ears. *What would Aunt Agatha do?* She cleared her throat, making effort to keep her voice from shaking. "May I introduce myself? I am Doctor Sherry Ramhill newly arrived from England."

The demon nodded her head and remained silent.

"Oh, yes, if I know your name, I should have some power over you. Am I correct?"

"Rubbish." The demon yawned. "Giving you my name enters into a social contract suggesting we might ultimately be friends."

"That would be lovely." Sherry smiled. "I do not have a demon friend, and I am certain there is much you could teach me. I have studied many species, but I don't believe there is any medical manual for demons."

"Why would there be? Mankind has little interest in healing demons. On the contrary, just as your little friends have demonstrated, killing is the agenda." The demon picked Christian up and shook him until he dropped the knife he had pulled from his boot.

"If you don't mind, I would prefer they were returned unbroken."

"Unbroken?" Demon laughter echoed through the cavern. "If the other one persists in smacking me with his sword, it will not be the only thing broken." The demon shifted, applying more weight.

"Nick, stop this instant." Sherry demanded.

His expletives died as he gasped for breath.

"Now, the one in your right claw is Christian McMillan and the one under your left leg is Nick Szabo. They are both lovely men when in a better mood."

"You're a funny one, Dr. Ramhill." The demon stretched out her sinuous neck and studied Sherry's face. Hot breath moved Sherry's hair. "Any relationship to Agatha Ramhill?"

147

"Why, yes, she is my aunt." Sherry stopped, putting her hand to her mouth. "Oh dear, is it a good thing?"

The demon laughed again, her wings settling behind her shoulders, "Certainly, she's a dear friend." Lifting her leg and using her long hind claws, she pushed Nick along the floor toward Sherry. He scrambled to his feet, rubbing his ribs. As he lifted the sword, Sherry placed her hand on his, stopping its ascent.

"Very good," the demon nodded. "I see you have some control over your companions."

Sherry eyed Nick. "Very little but I believe he will see the advantage to a conversation rather than another confrontation."

Nick snarled at her before nodding. Her mouth quirked at the edges, and she resisted the urge to say 'good boy'.

"And Christian?" Sherry inquired.

The demon lifted Christian and stared at him, her eyes narrowing. "I've heard stories about the McMillans. Don't know if he is from their clan." She sniffed his hair. "Smells like a priest." She commented as she set him on his feet and patted his back to move him toward the others.

"That's what Gino says." Nick mumbled.

Sherry shushed him. "May I be so bold as to ask why you are here?"

The demon raised one eye ridge at Sherry. She took in a deep breath and expelled it in a great sigh. "If you must know the truth, I'm hiding."

"From what?" Sherry wrinkled her brow. "A demon hunter?"

"Actually, another demon." Her body shrank two sizes. "I have committed a—well, I won't use the word mortal—but a sin against demon-kind or so she believes." She shrank a

148

little more and the wings disappeared into her shoulder blades. "And there are those who would punish me for it." Her front legs became arms and she stood on two legs, her skin losing the reptilian gray-green and flushing into pink. She sat on a rock and combed her fingers through silky black hair hanging to her knees, only partially covering an elegant lithe body.

Nick stared at the demon's elegant figure. Sherry elbowed him in the gut. She caught Christian the same on the forward swing. They shook themselves from the demon's spell.

"Are you a succubus?" Sherry found herself becoming mesmerized by the demon's rhythmic motion.

"Heavens, no." The demon shook her head. "I'm a much higher-level demon. Much more into corporate intrigue." The demon looked down. "Oh, I see why you ask. Let me put on something a little less revealing." She chuckled.

Disappearing behind the boulder, she returned a moment later, shook out a long dress and shimmied into it. The soft fabric did not hide her curves. "Now, tell me, what are you doing here? Out on a lark?"

"We are searching for what is causing the problems with the water system." Sherry pointed to the floating *teppichs*. "One *teppich* found its way to the river and was dining on a barge. This is not normal fare for this species. There must be many others about as they are disrupting the water handling for the city."

"Oh, dear. I'm afraid I've been unable to find the appropriate greens for them. Green plants don't grow well underground." The demon moved swiftly to the pool and rubbed the closest *teppich*. A loud purring filled the cavern.

She straightened, shrugged her shoulders and let out a sigh. "We've come this far, we might as well go all the way." The demon extended her hand to Sherry. "You may call me Letitia."

Sherry shook her hand, noting the warm, firm grip. "That means filled with joy in Latin, doesn't it?"

Letitia smiled, "Yes, it's a name given to me by someone special. He said I made him happy." She offered her hand to Christian and then to Nick. "I have been remiss. You're soaking wet and the temperature in the cave is a bit cool. Please, come into my living space." She walked around the large rock formation and disappeared. Light shone from the other side. Her voice emanated from the back. "Gentlemen, do leave your weapons at the door."

Sherry looked at each man who motioned for her to proceed. Rounding the boulder, she found a wall with a massive metal door. The doorway led to a large rectangular room hewn from the stone. Cherry paneling lined the walls to well above Christian's head. A four poster Elizabethan bed with burgundy brocade curtains stood in one corner. A double door wardrobe covered with intricate carving in dark walnut stood to the side. In the center, three overstuffed couches boxed a raised fireplace. Letitia waved them to the couches. Before Nick could take a seat, Letitia handed him a heavy woolen blanket. "If I had clothes to fit you, I'd be glad to share but your shoulders are too broad for anything in my closet. And the clothes left by the previous occupant have all gone to dust."

"This will do fine, ma'am." Nick pulled the blanket closer. He looked at the couch. Letitia handed another blanket to Christian and motioned for them to sit.

"Don't worry. It will dry." Letitia opened a mahogany captain's chest and handed Christian four cut glass tumblers. Rummaging deeper, she held up the decanter in triumph. "Knew I had it somewhere. Christian, please pour while I put on the kettle."

Christian accepted the decanter and poured two fingers for each. He set them on the marble edge of the firepit to warm. Letitia returned with a black iron kettle, the cunning

150

dragon's tail curled up into a handle. She hung it on an iron hook dangling from a spit and pushed the arm over the fire. She stared at the embers for a moment. The fire blossomed into open flame.

"Are you a fire demon, then?" Christian asked.

"No, not by any stretch. Small things like lighting fires are in every demon's repertoire." She eyed the tumblers then picked up one and carefully divided the contents into the others. She smiled at Sherry's scrutiny. "Yes, dear, I am." Her hand hovered over her abdomen. "While I doubt a little alcohol would hurt a demon child, this one is a demi-demon. So, I'm in hiding."

Sherry eyed the cognac. Christian handed a glass to her and Nick. Letitia opened a water bottle, filled her glass and held it up to salute them.

"Now, what are we going to do about this situation? I'm in hiding and I can't let you go out and tell folks I'm here." She leaned back.

Nick half rose from the couch, a dark scowl on his face. She waved him back down. "Now, we don't want to return to our earlier state, do we? While I am certain the you two are very proficient with your weapons, I still have you outclassed. And I don't want my living quarters in disarray."

Sherry laughed, drawing raised eyebrows from both men. "Gentlemen, this is obviously a situation for negotiation." She turned to Letitia. "How do you know my aunt?"

"Agatha? Why we have been … involved … several times in the past." She sipped the water.

"Involved?" Sherry, too, raised an eyebrow.

"No, nothing so interesting. If it is your Aunt's taste, I don't know about it. I've merely assisted her when she was a young vampire hunter."

Sherry pursed her lips. "I didn't know she ever was. She has always been ... old ... to me." Letitia studied her, amusement on her face. "Why are you in hiding?"

"Hecate prefers a monopoly on the spawning demi-demons. She's building her army. Doesn't like competition. She'd dispatch me on sight." She sighed. "And there are others who would kill this child just for spite. It's in their nature, you know." She looked at her empty glass. "But this isn't getting us any closer to a resolution."

A metallic screech emanated from deeper in the shadows behind them. A sound similar to windchimes continued for several heartbeats. Nick and Christian looked at each other.

"You might as well satisfy your curiosity. And see if you can stop the screech while you're at it. It has become rather annoying." She waved a hand in dismissal. "Sherry and I will continue toward a satisfactory compromise."

Nick dropped the blanket on the couch and stepped around the firepit. Christian joined him. At the far end, stones in the walls shed light on the path into another chamber. A large metal construction glowed with whirling lights. The metal frame sprouted long curved wires circling in slow rotation, small metal shapes dangling from each wire.

"I haven't seen one of these since I was in Birmingham." Christian said. "England ... not Alabama. It is in Thinktank, the Science Museum."

"What is it?" Nick ran a finger along the smooth strut.

"It looks like an Orrery ... it models the universe. Each globe represents a planet in accurate miniature size. The orbs rotate around the sun at a speed proportional to the planet's actual speed. But these aren't balls. They are misshapen." Christian walked around the device, eying the rotating arms and the shapes hanging from them. "There are too many arms ... too many for the planets." He backed away squinting his eyes.

"Christian, they're not planets. They're islands and countries." Nick pointed at the swinging shapes. "See? This is the British Isle and there goes Italy. China's coming around your way."

Christian identified the land masses as they rotated around the globe shape. "Some struts are damaged." He examined the broken ends. "I don't recognize the metal."

The whole construct shuddered twice, paused as Australia and Saudi Arabia tangled. The metal spines drew taut. Pulling apart, the screech replayed.

Christian ran his hands down the strut holding Australia. He pulled it lower, reshaping the curve in the wire. "There, it should swing free."

"Nick. Christian." Sherry called. The two men sprinted back to the living area, concern written on their faces. Sherry smiled at them and shook hands with Letitia. "We've come to an understanding. As long as we promise not to discuss her presence with anyone ..." She tapped a finger on each chest. "Then we are free to go."

"But we still have the drainage problem—" Christian interrupted.

"The only two people who can be privy to this information is Madam Miriam and Professor Lizzard. I am certain with their help, we can resolve that issues."

"And what price are you going to pay?" Nick glowered at her.

"Why, free pre-natal medical care." She glared back at him. "To rephrase an old movie line, I do know something about birthin' babies."

Christian laughed out loud at Sherry's abysmal southern accent.

"Gentlemen, on the way out, don't forget your toys."

Chapter Twenty

Dawson holds a meeting

"Alright, we've been at this for two days and have nothing to show for it!" Dawson Hughes stormed at his team.

"But, boss, we've had interference on all levels. Kids bugging us, the zoo dame moving animals around and the damn mayor coming up with antiquated ordinances ... like ... like a man with a lantern walking in front of the trucks when we go up the back roads behind the zoo." Sam looked around at the nodding heads.

"Well, suck it up! We've faced worse. What about the underwater temple with the sharks and moray eels? Didn't stop us from getting to that treasure." Dawson slammed his fist on the table. "Enough excuses."

He looked each man in the eye. Few met his angry stare. "Now, Sam, tell us again what emanations you recorded from the satellite ... why we're in this backwater town."

"Uh ... it's an old artifact sitting on or near a crossing of the leylines. The emanations are weak... most likely in underground cave, not just buried near the surface. The best location I can tell from the data is somewhere about five miles north." He looked at Dawson and hurried on before he could question him. "But with the cave structure and the old water systems, there could be echoes ... which makes it harder to pinpoint."

Dawson looked at each man. "Okay, so what we know is there's an old sewer system flowing to the water treatment plant. The storm drains capture the flow that area into an old cistern. Probably the detritus hasn't been cleaned out in a century. Or—" he looked around the room again. "Something is attracted to the artifact which is clogging the drains. Eric, you've been down there. What did you find?"

"Besides feeling like I was being watched the whole time," he shivered. "I found a swimming creature with long hair acting like a shop vac and eating everything in sight. The odd thing is it belched a Sulphur smell. And believe me, it has buzz saw teeth."

"Go on," Dawson cleaned his nails with his pocket knife, not looking up.

"A bunch could clog the system." Eric cleared his throat. "There are definitely others living down there. There's got to be."

"I don't care about subterranean dwellers—we've run into them before—glorified street scum. What I need from you is a quick strike and we can leave. What's the best guess and how do we get there?" He gestured to the map on the table. Each man pointed a finger at his chosen spot. Three fingers found the same area, beyond the water treatment plant and the zoo.

"Okay, much better. Now how do we get there?"

The youngest man raised his hand.

"Nate, you aren't in high school anymore. You don't need to raise your hand." Dawson grinned at him.

"Okay, Boss. So, I talked to the high school kids. Yeah, this baby face helps out sometimes. They say there's a tunnel. Leads from the sewage plant into the cave system. Haunted … or guarded by weird creatures … or whatever other horror story you want to hear. It's a local dare to go in. Those who've tried find their flashlights useless about 20 yards in."

"Could be the artifact's effect on electrical items. Good work." Dawson pointed to the sewage plant. "We go in tomorrow night. Find the artifact. Then we can get back to civilization." Dawson dismissed them but stopped Nate with a hand on his shoulder.

Gene pulled on his raincoat. "Sam, you promised me there was a good bar in town. Last night, I just wanted to hide under a blanket in a locked room. This time, I need a beer."

Sam looked back at Dawson who had his head together with Nate. "Shhh, I don't think the Boss would appreciate our rubbing elbows with the locals."

"Aww, come on. Since when does he scare you?" Gene jabbed his elbow in Sam's ribs.

"Since forever." Sam stepped out the door. "But okay, I need one, too. It's down the street by the waterfront."

***

Sherry slipped up to the back door, removed her muddy boots and left them on the porch. *One good thing about pixies*, she thought, *they like things neat and tidy*. She knew her boots would be clean in the morning. *Extra butterscotch for this mess.* She laughed under her breath then squeaked when Miasma rubbed against her ankle.

Miasma, don't scare me like that!

Then pay better attention to your surroundings. You are wanted in the parlor.

I'm not even in the door yet. How does she know I'm home?

Silly question. Miasma leapt onto the kitchen countertop. She nudged a tin with her paw. *Please open the sardines before you go in.*

Sherry pulled the ring opening the tin. She looked at the sharp edge then retrieved a small bowl from the cabinet. The sardines slipped into the bowl. Miasma put both paws on the edge and guided Sherry's hand to the counter.

Mmmhrrr. Miasma gathered a sardine into her mouth, slurping it up.

"I'll interpret the sound as a thank you." Sherry said and pushed through the swinging door to the hall.

"Sherry, dear, we're in here." Madam's voice came from the front parlor.

"Yes, ma'am. I am rather dusty. Let me change and I will be right down." She placed her bare foot on the stairs.

"Sherry, please. The dust will clean up. I have a guest I would like you to meet."

Sherry paused. *A guest? But I look a fright.* She sighed and stepped to the parlor door. A young woman dressed in a long olive-green skirt with a cream blouse embroidered with trailing vines and gold bell flowers stood by the side table. Her long black hair in a braid trailed over one shoulder, tip brushing a large moonstone set in warm gold hanging around her neck.

"Sherry, I would like you to meet Triss Fairhaven, the Mayor's wife." Madam sat in her wingback chair by the fire.

Triss stepped forward, her hand held out. Sherry was surprised by her warmth and strength. Before she could help herself, she blurted out, "Is he real? I mean I haven't managed to catch him in his office at all this week." Sherry blushed at her audacity.

Triss laughed while Madam scowled at Sherry. "Yes, Dr. Ramhill, he is real, but he doesn't like to be confined. You're more likely to catch him walking the beat as the foot police say. My husband is deeply invested in growing this

158

community particularly the area around Baker Street. He has hopes for an artist's colony."

"Forgive my rudeness." Sherry apologized. "It has been a long day."

Triss handed Sherry a plate from the side table. "That is why I brought you some dinner. I suspect your escapades did not include food. Cook is off today."

Sherry stared at the three perfect, warm perogies topped with sour cream, bacon and cheddar cheese.

"Sherry, for goodness sake, sit down and eat." Madam held up her stemmed glass to which Triss added a deep red wine. Pouring a second glass, she handed it to Sherry then motioned her to the other wingback chair. Triss sat on the loveseat with her feet tucked up under her, a wine glass in her hand.

Sherry juggled the plate. Her mouth watered at the aroma. She took up the fork and ate slowly while Madam and Triss conversed about various people in town. Sherry surmised Triss had been away for a time. As she finished the meal, she wondered if Miasma could teach her to purr. The Syrah burned her throat so pleasantly.

"Now, my dear, please tell us about your latest adventure." Madam looked in Sherry's direction.

"Oh, it was nothing. Just exploring the caves down by the sewage plant." Sherry sipped on her wine, her eyes averted.

"I am certain there is something more exciting. Why don't you tell us what you found?" Madam persevered.

"Madam, I gave my word I would only tell you and Professor Lizzard." She looked at Triss. "No offense intended. Seems to be the only thing I can say tonight."

Madam's face went ashen. "Don't speak that name in this house." She emptied her glass and held it out. Before Triss could rise, Sherry leapt to her feet and refilled the glass. She turned to Triss who also raised her glass.

"Madam, I don't know why you have such an aversion to the Professor. He is a perfect gentleman." Sherry refilled her own glass. "After all, you are on the City Council with him."

"And as close as I will ever get to him is the council table's far end. I forbid you to mention him again. Enough." Madam's lips thinned to a single line.

"I just don't—" Sherry caught a movement in her peripheral vision. She glanced at Triss who shook her head. Sherry bit back her next words and sat down, drowning in the silence.

Miasma entered the door, belly to the floor and ears laid back. She slunk along the baseboard until she was beside Madam's chair. A single leap levitated her into Madam's lap. Her lawnmower purr filled the room. Madam stroked Miasma's back. Within a few moments, Madam took a deep shuddering breath and turned to look at Sherry.

"You may speak freely no matter your promise. I trust Triss with my life. Not something I will say about many. And her council is wise." Madam straightened her spine challenging Sherry to defy her.

Sherry bit her tongue.

"Good. You're learning." Miasma touched her thoughts.

"We met Letitia … who happens to be a demon and is living in the cave beyond the zoo." She waited for her words to sink in.

"Letitia?" Madam's voice regained its lilt. "I remember your Aunt mentioning her several years ago. Go on, dear. Why is she here?"

Sherry took a deep breath and recounted the tale from the beginning. When she described the very short battle between

160

Nick and Christian with the full demon manifestation, Triss laughed so hard she had to hold on so she wouldn't fall off the loveseat. Madam wiped tears from her eyes with her silk handkerchief. The atmosphere in the room lightened and Sherry relaxed.

"I have promised to help her with her baby." She yawned. "Please forgive me. This has been cathartic, and it has worn me out."

Triss rose. She kissed Madam on the cheek and gave Sherry a hug. "You will sleep deeply and arise refreshed. We have much to discuss tomorrow." She wrapped her fringed shawl around her shoulders.

Sherry yawned again but she stood quickly. "Let me drive you home."

"Thank you for the offer but Arnie is waiting for me outside. He will see me safely home." She looked at Madam. "And to bed with you as well, Madam."

Sherry took Madam's arm and the two climbed the stairs. At her bedroom door, Madam kissed Sherry's forehead. "Triss is never wrong about a good night's sleep." She opened her door and shut it behind her.

Miasma wound around Sherry's ankles. She picked up the cat and nuzzled her fur. Together, they sought the warmth under the counterpane. *Who ... or what ... is Triss? How can she talk to Madam in such a way?* Her eyes closed and did not open until morning.

***

"Professor Lizzard, I am so glad you could join us." Nick offered his hand as the Professor descended the outer stairs. He held the door open for the gentleman to enter the bar.

"This is a refreshing change, my friend. I haven't been in here for a very long time." He inhaled deeply. "And Madrecita is filling the air with the most delicious aroma!"

161

Nick led Vincent to a table in the back. Before he could seat himself, Gino arrived with a beer mug. "Ah, Gino, my dear boy, you are just in time." He accepted the mug and took a long drink. "Bluetongue. Outstanding. My favorite and it does match my tongue." Vincent unrolled his tongue and wagged it at Gino. In the dim light, it was clearly a blue gray.

Gino grimaced. "The Boss ordered it specifically for you."

"He did?" Vincent looked at Nick who smiled at him. "Well, then, I will have to frequent this establishment more often. Can't survive on the cookies the young zoo director brings."

Micah materialized at the Professor's elbow with a large bowl containing fish chowder and two softball-sized wheatberry rolls. Setting it on the table, he offered a spoon. The Professor accepted with a nod.

"How are you doing with the new director, Micah?"

"Very well, sir. She is slowly learning the ropes. She would be fully oriented if she didn't keep running off with these two." He ducked a cuff from Nick and escaped the backhand offered by Christian as he stepped away from the table.

"Professor, we explored the cave system beyond the sewage treatment plant. We were sworn to secrecy except for you and Madam Miriam. I'm sure Sherry's filling her in as we speak."

"Then you must have found something very interesting. The brimstone's source, perhaps?" He peered at each in turn. "You are feeling quite well, are you not?"

"Quite, sir. Letitia—the demon—explained she came through a portal from the third level—she was running away and it was open so she just jumped through. It opened into the caves. Once here, she closed the portal." Christian explained as Vincent finished the chowder and the second roll.

Vincent choked, then cleared his throat. "Then Nigel and I were right. Absolutely wonderful!"

"She said the brimstone in the cave has dropped considerably since her arrival."

"Then why are we still detecting it?" Vincent furrowed his brow then slapped his forehead. "The *teppich*. Their thick fur must have absorbed it and it will take time for it to work its way out. Poor Alighieri, he was tracking the *teppichs*— probably too much exposure to them." He emptied his mug and studied the bottom with a sad look on his face. Nick signaled Gino.

"Professor, there was something more interesting in the cave." Christian waited for Gino to leave the fresh mug.

"More interesting than a demon? My boy, you have an unusual viewpoint." Vincent nodded for him to go on.

"I've seen my share, Professor. But I've only seen one orrery which isn't of the planets." Christian pulled out his cell phone. "I didn't want to invade her privacy but this was here before Letitia moved in." He held up the picture.

Vincent peered at the image. "Interesting. I'd have to see it up close but it does resemble an orrery. But you say they are not planets?"

Christian chuckled, "They're countries"

"Countries? How curious. Is it functional? I see broken ends here in the corner."

"Partially. It is still trying to turn but some areas hang up until the force is great enough to overcome the resistance. I've tweaked it for now." Christian flipped to another image. "And the outer room is furnished with an Elizabethan-style bed, writing desk, and a large wardrobe. Expensive wood paneling. The whole places swirls with old magick … weak but definitely there. Someone was living there before the demon arrived."

"Gentlemen, you may have found the illusive device to balance the leylines. Nigel will eat his hat when he sees these pictures." Vincent bounced in his seat.

"Professor," Nick laid a hand on his arm to slow the motion. "We promised to keep her existence a secret. She is in hiding for reasons Sherry can better explain."

"Certainly, but I have to see this device for myself." He looked from one to the other. "Can it be arranged?"

Nick and Christian looked at each other. "We'd best leave the negotiation to Sherry."

"Very well then. I will speak with her first thing in the morning." Vincent yawned. "My apologies but this has been too much excitement for my old bones. I will bid you good night." He stood and half bowed to them. "Thank you for giving me much to think about."

His tall frame disappeared up the outer steps and into the night.

"Mr. Nick?" Micah stood at Nick's shoulder. "See those two in the corner?"

Nick turned slightly to view the two men at the far table.

The younger man held the other by the arm and pulled him to his feet. "Gene, you've had too much to drink. Shut up or Dawson will have you for breakfast. Enough talk." He half carried Gene up the stairs and into the street.

"The older man said he didn't want to go into the caves— that they are haunted. The other one said it was Dawson's order. He also said, 'Tomorrow night, we can get away from here.' I noticed his coat said Santos Development."

164

"Good job, Micah." Nick said. "Looks like we will be talking with Dr. Ramhill tomorrow, too."

Chapter Twenty-One

Sherry and Arnie hatch a plan

Sherry walked down the path past the koi pond, lost in thought regarding Nick's news. *What are we going to do about the Santos men?* She kicked a stone in the pathway. *They won't go away easily*, she thought. She picked it up to skip across the pond then decided not to when the koi gathered at the surface attracted by her shadow. She tossed it over her shoulder.

"Ow." The deep voice sounded amused rather than in pain, but she turned around quickly. Finding the path empty, she peered carefully at the bushes.

"Micah, are you playing with me?"

No answer.

Wrinkling her forehead, she sat down on the rock outcropping preparing to return to her thoughts. She smoothed the front of her khaki pants easing the cuffs over her boots.

"Dr. Ramhill, I've wanted to get to know you better but Chazel won't approve you sitting on my lap."

Sherry jumped up and swung around just in time to watch Arnie morph out from what she thought was a large stone into his seven-foot frame complete with wings unfurled.

166

"Arnie, you scared the bloomers off me." She wiped her face with her handkerchief. Arnie gently took her arm and led her to the marble bench overlooking the pond. She bent her knees to sit then shot upright. She looked at the bench. "A relative?"

Arnie laughed, his deep voice rolling like thunder in the distance. "No, I assure you. This one is real marble." He sat down and patted the space beside him.

Sherry sank down and heaved a sigh. "What were you doing sitting there?" She waved her handkerchief at the crushed grass by the walk.

"Waiting for Greg. He's checking on the bees. I don't like the little stingers." Arnie pulled a small bag from his pocket and tossed green peas into the pond. The water roiled with the large koi.

"Oh," Sherry paused searching for the correct words. "I read a bit about your people whilst in school. I didn't realize you could change shape."

"It is a bit childish but when I'm lonely, I go back to the basics—the boulder I was before I grew into this." Arnie waved his hand at his frame.

"Lonely? Are you all alone? Was there a tragedy?" She patted his stony hand.

Arnie's laugh grumbled scaring the fish. "No disaster. My family are all here."

"What? Well, where are they? I've not seen anyone but you and Chaszel."

Arnie pulled out his wallet. "Here's the cathedral." He held out the photograph. "My uncle Andre up there. My Ma on the other side."

167

"Will they come down and meet me?" Sherry said.

"No, Dr. Ramhill. They don't like to talk. They say I talk enough for all the Gargoyles."

"Could I go up and talk to them?"

"You could but they would only listen." Arnie folded the wallet and tucked it away.

"But you are lonely for them?"

"No, I miss Dr. Alighieri. He was teaching me Italian. I want to visit the Gargoyles in Rome. They are my oldest relatives." Arnie's face pulled down in a long pout.

"I speak some Italian. I'd be glad to share what little I know." She chuckled. "It's mainly how to order delicious food."

"Dr. Ramhill, you're most kind and it would lighten my heart. Thank you. But you were wearing a thoughtful face as you walked up here. Is there anything I can do?" Arnie's sincere look touched Sherry.

"First, please call me Sherry. Second, we've found out the Santos Corporation men are treasure hunters. We have to find a way to send them packing but not expose the …occupant in the cave."

"Someone's living there again?" Arnie asked.

"Again? Then you know who was there before?" Wind blew leaves around her feet, startling her. Arnie put an arm around her shoulders. She looked up at his face, then beyond him to the gathering clouds, their grey color ominous.

"So my great grandmother says, but she is a bit addled since she fell off the cathedral roof. No one else ever saw the fellow she described. She said he was young until he was old. Very personable. Liked to sit on the cathedral's roof at night and launch sparks from his fingertips." Arnie stood. "But she is rather daft." He stretched. "Sherry, I need to walk, or I will become as the marble bench. Shall we?"

Arnie's dinner plate-sized grasp swallowed her hand. She rose with his gentle pull.

"There is a new occupant and she wants to stay hidden. But we are sure the Santos men will be poking around in the caves tonight for a magical item we really don't want them to find."

"In the caves? And you want to scare them away?" Arnie laid a finger by his nose and grinned, his eyes flashing. "I've an idea and I'm certain the wererats and the trolls will want in on the fun."

"What do you have in mind?" Sherry cocked her head, staring at him.

"The clans do a wonderful job on the haunted house each year for Halloween. It won't be hard to haunt the caves." Arnie's grin widened. "You find a decoy magical item and we'll send them running."

He held up his hand for a high five. Sherry stretched up on tip toe, slapped his hand then blew on it to take away the sting.

***

"Mr. Mayor?" Jonas opened the inner office door. Yancy looked up from the Santos Development proposal scattered across his desk. Jonas winced.

"Jonas, this is bogus. There has to be a flaw in here which will void this agreement. Markus won't be any help." He grabbed up his coffee cup, muttering it was empty.

"Mr. Mayor. Mr. Szabo and Mr. McMillan are here to see you."

169

"What? Nick? Now?" He looked at his watch. It was nearly noon. The Breitling's square face soothed him. His grandfather proudly wore it during WWI. *What would he do in this situation? Stand tall and tell the City Council no. If they balked, he would call a referendum by the voters. Not a bad idea.*

"Jonas, draw up a referendum regarding the Santos proposal, and call an emergency council meeting for tomorrow evening." Yancy heaved a sigh. "And would you mind a refill?" Yancy held up his cup.

Nick nudged past Jonas. Yancy stood and came around the desk to offer his hand. "Nick, I believe this is the first time you have ever come to my office."

"I hope it'll be the last time it's necessary. We have information but it needs to remain confidential."

"Information? Regarding?" Yancy frowned.

"The Santos Development and more specifically what they are here for … and it isn't to build a resort." Nick grabbed Yancy's elbow and steered him toward the door. "There's a meeting in the bar and you're needed." He grabbed the coat from the coat rack and threw it over Yancy's shoulder.

Jonas stared as the two exited the office. He jumped when he caught movement in his peripheral vision. "Mr. McMillan, I forgot you were still here."

"Here's your coat, Jonas." He tossed the coat in the air. "You and I have lots to talk about." Christian stepped into the hallway. "Come on."

Jonas eyebrows rose on his forehead. "Me?"

Christian nodded.

Jonas snatched up his keys and locked the door, hurrying down the stairs.

Sherry looked from face to face. "So, we now know the Santos Development is a front and their men are in reality treasure hunters … specifically for items with magical power. Professor Lizzard is convinced the item Christian discovered is a mechanical device meant to regulate energy in the ley lines. Professor?"

Lizzard stood and looked around the table. "I have inspected the device and it is very significant. It does match the descriptions. It also is emanating a magical aura consistent with the Merlins." Heads nodded around the room. "Someone was living there for quite a while and had excellent taste in furnishings. I conjecture it was the Merlin tending the instrument, but he has been gone a long time for the magical aura to be so weak."

"Professor?" Chaszel rolled the marble sounds in her mouth. "Is it what the treasure hunters are seeking?"

"My best guess." Lizzard answered in the same dialect.

"Your accent is improving, Vincent." Chaszel complimented. Lizzard inclined his head in thanks and to hide a lump in his throat.

"But the energy flowing through the ley lines is already weak. Wouldn't removing the device further diminish the flow?" Madrecita inquired.

"Most likely." Sherry jumped in. "So, we have to find a way to hide it."

"Water." Sherry turned to find the soft voice. Triss stood at the far end, her hand on Yancy's shoulder. Sherry noted his bright smile as he looked up at his wife. "Water will disrupt the magical aura and render it nearly undetectable. The deeper the water, the more the aura will be dampened."

"Will water damage the device?" Anastasia asked. She nodded at Gregariel knowing his fascination with all things mechanical.

"My question, exactly." He grinned back at her.

Professor Lizzard found his voice. "Most likely not. Though I do not understand the workings, its constituents are inert metals. As it is already functioning poorly, there will be significant work needed to restore it. A bath shouldn't do any harm."

Sherry called their attention. "There is one more issue."

All eyes turned in her direction.

"The cave is occupied. The current resident has done us a service. When she came to this plane, she did so through a portal from Hell. She closed the portal behind her, stopping the brimstone pouring in." Sherry hurried on before consternation could erupt. "Already the *teppichs* are returning to their normal habitat and they are no longer carrying the brimstone on their fur ... or their breath."

"But a demon!" Yancy spoke for the first time. "Isn't she dangerous to us all?" He put his hand over Triss'.

Madam appeared on his other side. "You have every right to be concerned, Mr. Mayor. But in this case, I am confident she is not a threat. I wished to speak to the young woman myself before I could vouch for her." Murmuring broke out around the table but quickly hushed by Madam's wave. "I assure you her motives are quite innocent. She is, in effect, seeking asylum."

"I support Madam's evaluation," Sherry said drawing herself up to her full height. "We need to find her a safe place to hide while we deal with the Santos men."

"Can't the Mayor just tell them to leave?" Arnie asked.

Everyone turned to Yancy. He cleared his throat. "This is a delicate matter. There are members on the City Council who are not believers in magic nor your community's existence. They would not understand the reason for such a request. And they would call the authorities in white coats if I told them there was a demon involved. They're blinded by the offer to solve the problems with the water systems."

"Well put, Yancy." Madam acknowledged. "I believe Arnie has a solution."

"Okay, if we can create sufficient hurdles for them, they'll take a decoy item in their haste to get away from the caves." He turned to Sherry. "Dr. Ramhill ... er... Sherry will obtain such an item." She nodded in agreement. He looked at Marty then at Greg. "There is a role for all our clans." He spread his arms wide. "And anyone else who wishes to have a little fun. Remember the haunted house last Halloween? Well, I think we can do even better." He grinned, his white teeth gleaming.

Chapter Twenty-Two
Sherry visits Granny's Attic

"Sherry, it's time you met another friend in our community."
Madam held out her hand to Triss. She worked her way
through the individuals leaving the table. Some were intent
on shaking the Mayor's hand which made the travel
upstream challenging. When the three were together, Madam
led the way up the stairs to the street.

"Fortunately, the weather is clear at the moment." She
eyed the clouds on the horizon in the west. "But it looks to
be a rainy night. Just the right ambience for Arnie's hijinks."
All three laughed at the glee on his face when he proposed
the evening's escapade.

Madam led them down Bridge Street and then took a right
onto Baker Street. As they strolled farther from the river, the
warehouses gave way to store fronts with apartments on the
second floor. The walls were red brick with quaint dentil
work and wrought iron filigree on the windows. One shop
stood out from the others with massive window boxes on
both large front windows and planters on the sidewalk. Each
overflowed with riotous colorful blooms. The sun shone
brightly on the door while other doors were partially hidden
in gloom. The yellow and gold sign above the door
announced "Granny's Attic."

Madam pushed open the door, a crystalline chime
announcing their arrival. The scent greeting them recalled

174

warmth and comfort. Sherry smiled, not certain why she felt happy.

"Mimi, darling, do come in and bring your new charge." The voice matched the scent, welcoming and embracing. Madam escorted them past the shelves filled with exotic spices and incense from all over the world, shining brass temple bowls and cymbals, the windchimes each sending out a sonic snippet and through a bamboo curtain. Beyond opened into a large workroom with a kitchen at one end and two long stainless-steel tables dividing the room.

Madam rushed into the arms of a short, stout woman, her age indeterminate. Her white hair glistened in the sunshine through the large window. She stood on tiptoe to kiss Madam on the cheek, her deep blue eyes glittering.

Madam released her from a tight hug and turned to the others. "Granny, this is Sherry Ramhill, the new director for the zoo."

"Dear, I heard about poor Dante. I warned him not to trace the brimstone without protection." She held out a hand to Sherry who leapt forward to take it. Warmth suffused her when skin met skin. Granny held onto her hand and pulled her to the table in the kitchen alcove. The scent of freshly brewed peppermint tea filled the air.

"I have cinnamon scones just out. Everyone, sit." She pulled plates from the open shelves above the countertop and put a scone on each, handing them to Triss, and motioning toward the table. "And just for you, Sherry, I have clotted cream." Opening the refrigerator, she retrieved a small white crock and a jar of raspberry jam. "Now tell me, do you eat it ala Cornwall or Devon?"

Triss looked at Sherry with a question in her eyes.

"In Cornwall, the first dollop is jam followed by the cream and in Devon, it is cream first with jam second." Sherry colored a little in her cheeks. "I prefer Devon style as it is the cream I crave." She plucked up the crock and added a heaping spoonful to her scone. Madam handed her the jam, a twinkle in her eye as she met Sherry's. A smaller spoon ladled out the required jam. Sherry nibbled at the edge then bit into the scone with a sigh. "This is heaven sent."

"My dear, I am so glad you like it. I've had it ready for a while, anticipating your visit." She turned to Madam. "Mimi, what has taken you so long to bring her in for introductions?"

Madam looked away, unwilling to meet Granny's eye. Sherry noticed Madam's deference to the smaller woman.

"I have been very busy what with the flooding problems." Sherry hurried on. "I have met some very interesting people. The Mayor, Jonas, Nick and Christian and Profes—"

Before she could go any further, Granny placed a hand on her arm. "That's lovely, dear. The important thing is you are here now." Granny looked from Madam to Triss. "And we should get on about the reason you're here." Granny stood.

Sherry noticed the table was clear but she had not seen anyone rise.

She looked at Triss who nodded, smiling. "Come, let's join Granny at the worktable." She held out her hand to Madam.

"You go ahead. I will gather the herbs I need." Madam returned to the front.

"Now then, Triss, what does the party need?" Granny tied on a white floor-length apron.

"An item with enough magick aura to be mistaken for the artifact they seek." Triss handed Sherry an apron and donned her own.

"Artifact? Something with a magical aura?" Granny rummaged through a large wardrobe which teetered alarmingly as she moved items about.

Sherry stood close by, ready to pull Granny out if the monstrous furniture chose to overturn. "The Santos men are really treasure hunters. But Professor ..." Sherry coughed and stole a glance at the bamboo curtain. "He says the device we've found is important for maintaining the leylines and we best not let them take it away."

"Ah hah!" She pulled a large, ornate metal vase from the dark interior. Lugging it to the table, she set it down with a loud clunk.

"There. This should do. It really is quite old which will make it interesting to a treasure hunter. But we will have to imbue it with the correct aura if it is to appear magical." Granny dropped into a chair at the table. "Do come sit."

Triss filled a glass with water and set it at Granny's right hand. She motioned to Sherry to take the chair on the left. Granny snatched up the glass and downed it. "Heavy work. The wardrobe doesn't give up its pretties without a struggle." Her throaty laughed rippled over them. The vase wobbled in time.

"Now, dear, let me see your hand." Granny held out her hand for Sherry's. She turned it palm up and peered at the lines.

"This is the second time this week, I've had my palm read." Sherry giggled.

Granny sat up straight, squeezing Sherry's hand tightly. Her eyes glittered, concern in them. "By whom? Who else has looked at your hand?"

Sherry stammered. "Christian ... Christian McMillan. I'm sure he was just flirting with me."

Granny's shoulders relaxed. "Christian. He's a dear boy. But—" She pulled Sherry close and spoke directly into her face. "Don't let folks be looking at your private information. It might lead to a bad end." She looked again at Sherry's palm. "Ah, the Ramhill dragon. Deeply etched. That's a good sign."

Sherry looked over Granny's silver white hair at Triss. Triss nodded, her face solemn.

"Alright then. It's definitely there. We can proceed." Granny squeezed Sherry's hand and released it. She pulled the metal vase closer.

"Forgive me, Granny, but what's there?" Sherry cocked her head to one side.

"The mark, dear. You definitely have your mother's magick inheritance ... in addition to your family's checkered history. But more about that later. Time is of the essence." Granny pulled a cloth from her pocket and rubbed the vase.

"No, I don't. There is not any magic in the family."

Granny handed the cloth to Triss who continued polishing. Turning her chair to face Sherry, she looked her up and down. "You look so much like young Agatha. Now, don't tell me you do not know Agatha's talents."

"Aunt Agatha was not allowed in the house after my mother died. My father insisted it was her influence which led to my mother's death. We weren't allowed to see her or even mention her." Sherry studied her fingernails, fighting back a lump in her throat.

"My poor dear." Granny squeezed her hand.

The lump untangled. Sherry sighed, feeling the tight knot around her heart unraveling as well.

"That is a shame ... for many reasons. I'm quite certain your mother's magic wasn't the problem ... rather your

178

father's obsession." Her voice stroked Sherry, soothing down the hurt. "But we haven't time to go into it right now." Sherry looked up at her, protest on her lips. Granny placed her warm finger on Sherry's lips. "We have an immediate issue. I promise we'll visit much more in the future. Trust me, you do have the magick in you."

She pulled Sherry's hand to the vase. "Do you feel anything?"

Sherry studied the vase, looking at it with the sight Madam opened for her. But it was still a vase. "No."

"Good. Because there isn't anything there." Granny laughed.

Sherry's forehead wrinkled. *Is she teasing me or laughing at me?*

"Neither, my dear. I merely wanted you to have a baseline and to see if you would imagine something in order to please me. I'm delighted with your forthright approach." She turned to Triss. "Will you please add a little something?"

Triss nodded and placed both hands on the vase. She closed her eyes, took a deep breath and exhaled. Sherry stared at Triss' hands. They took on a glow even in the workroom's bright light, the glow echoed in the large moonstone around her neck. After three breaths, Triss removed her hands and the glow faded.

"Now, Sherry. Try again to sense the magic in the vase." Granny smiled at her.

Of course, I will sense something. I've been pre-programmed to, she thought but she reached out. "Ow!" She pulled her hand back. "It shocked me."

"My apologies, I should have warned you about Triss' alignment with lightning. However, it does demonstrate you're more sensitive than you believe. If you weren't, you would just have felt the vase to be warmer than it was before.

179

This is wonderful. We must spend more time together." Granny grabbed a hand of each woman and pulled them to the vase. "Now to work."

"I don't know what to do." Sherry tried to pull back but Granny held firm.

"Close your eyes."

Sherry did as she was told.

"No peeking. Now, see the light behind your eyelids. Look for a spark … a firefly in the darkness. I know you see them." Granny's voice faded into a whisper. "Pretend the little spark is a paint brush. Now cover the vase with the beautiful light. Make it glow."

Granny's whisper echoed in Sherry's mind. She sighed but followed the instructions and imagined the spark painting the vase. It grew brighter until she wanted to close her eyes against the light. *But they are already closed!* She opened her eyes.

Granny said no peeking. Miasma rubbed against Sherry's leg. Sherry glanced down. She nearly laughed out loud. Miasma's fur stood out in all directions.

Are you everywhere or are you quintuplets?

I'm everywhere I'm supposed to be.

"Hehem." Granny cleared her throat. Sherry shut her eyes tight and once again, looked for the fireflies. There were now so many and they danced so fast, she barely caught one. Quickly she finished her third of the vase.

"Well then. You may open your eyes." Granny turned the vase all the way around. "Despite the interruption, we've done a good job."

Sherry felt her face warm from her throat up.

Triss handed her water, finished her own and set another beside Granny. Granny once again emptied the glass and set it down firmly on the table.

"Thirsty work, magic is." She chuckled. "Now I sound like Yoda." She pushed back her chair and stood, stretching her back, loud popping sounding through the workroom. "Well done. It isn't perfect but it'll attract those who are hunting."

Madam stood in the doorway, a large canvas bag over her shoulder. She handed it to Triss who scooped the vase in without touching it. "I assume you smudged the imprints, Granny."

"Of course, I did, Mimi. This isn't my first rodeo." Granny swept across the floor and pulled Madam into a tight embrace. Madam melted into Granny's arms. "All will be well. We'll save the zoo and all your friends."

"I've left payment on the counter." Madam motioned for Sherry to follow her as she stepped into the showroom.

Triss handed Sherry the bag. "Don't let anyone touch the vase. Place it somewhere away from any water."

Sherry felt the joined magic leaking through the bag. It tickled her fingers. She hurried into the next room to find Madam already at the front entrance. "Coming," she called then looked back through the bamboo curtain for Granny. The workroom was empty.

"She's gone to feed the cats in the courtyard. Every cat in town knows when she goes out." Triss walked with her to the front. "Don't worry. She knows you'll be back." Triss flipped the open sign to closed and slipped the lock on the door as they exited. She half bowed to Madam and walked in the bright sunlight toward home.

Sherry studied her graceful gait and smiled when Yancy appeared at the corner. His face shone brighter than the sunlight. He held out his arm and together, they walked away.

Madam raised a hand and a blue Lexus LX pulled to the curb. Micah took the bag from Sherry and tucked it in the back. He handed Madam into the back seat and held the door for Sherry.

"A man of many talents," she said. "Thank you."

Micah nodded, doffing his imaginary cap.

Chapter Twenty-Three

The Clans have a haunting good time

"Letitia is at Professor Lizzard's observatory?" Sherry held Christian's hand as she stepped from the dinghy. Once she was steady, he hauled the canvas bag onto the dock. He pushed the dinghy out of sight under the dock, looping the rope over the protruding hook.

"Yes, Professor was adamant he needed to see the orrery for himself so we took him to the caves. Armed with ginger cookies, I might add." He laughed at Sherry's quizzical expression. "The Professor suggested ginger is sufficiently hot a spice to be to a demon's liking … particularly a lady demon. And especially if she has been in hiding and not able to obtain the luxuries."

He opened the door to the sewage plant and motioned for her to proceed. She stepped onto the gangway, holding on to the railings on either side. The setting sun cast weak light through the doorway.

"The Professor is very charming and soon, they were laughing like old friends. When he suggested an opportunity to see the stars since it is going to be a clear night for once, she jumped at the chance." He tied a rope to the bag and lowered it to the floor below before climbing down the ladder. Sherry followed.

"Nick drove them up to the observatory. She insisted she was more comfortable with him than me. I have no idea why." His laughter echoed against the stone walls. He pulled on the heavy metal door.

Sherry studied him in the dim light. "Is it true?"

"What?" He shoved the door wide and picked up the bag.

"Are you a priest?"

"Was." His muffled reply reached her ears at the same time he entered the darkness. A flashlight snapped on. "Without Letitia here, I hope the light will function."

"I doubt it." Sherry mumbled as she hurried behind him. "Was?"

"Long story … best told over a good Scotch." His long legs carried him farther from her.

She trotted behind him, the light from her flashlight bobbing along. "What about the orrery?"

His voice carried back down the tunnel. "We dragged it into the pool. Professor fashioned a pallet for it so we can retrieve it later."

"Will the water damage it?" She caught up with him just as both flashlights flickered out.

"He doesn't think so. The orrery has been in this damp environment for some time, and there isn't any rust or corrosion." Christian set the sack on the floor and pulled a small torch from his backpack.

"Let me try," Sherry said. "Hold it out." Sherry wove her fingers in between his on the base. She closed her eyes and looked for the fireflies. Gathering a couple together, she directed them to the torch's tip. Light shone through her eyelids.

"Good work." Christian smiled at her, the reddish highlights in his hair gleaming in the firelight. He held the torch above his head and entered the large cavern.

"You won't need that." Triss' voice came from behind Sherry's shoulder.

Sherry whipped around, her eyes wide. "Where did you come from?"

"I've been standing right here." Taking Sherry by the elbow, she guided her into the alcove to the right. She placed Sherry's hand on the wall, her own hand on top. The dim grey glow brightened to green, illuminating the cavern.

"How did you do that?" Sherry turned to see Triss' face.

"Professor told me the key. The walls are covered in algae. It just needs a little nudge to glow. The algae are bioluminescent."

"How long will it glow?" Christian stepped up behind them.

"Naturally, about ten minutes. Then they slowly fade." Triss touched the wall again and the cavern descended into darkness. "They also respond to energy withdrawal."

A corresponding glow grew at the far end. Christian reached for his quarterstaff. Triss placed a hand on his arm. "Don't worry. Anastasia is practicing, too. She's delighted with this new ability." Triss led them into the main cavern. "Everyone's in place."

"What about the vase?" Sherry pointed at the bag. Arnie appeared from the shadows and picked it up. He held his hand out to Sherry. He led her to a dark area away from the water pool but visible from the tunnel's end. Handing her the bag, he lifted two middle sized boulders and shuffled smaller stone away with his feet. He nodded at the spot. Sherry opened the bag and rolled the vase out on its side, careful not to touch the surface. Arnie kicked smaller stones around it and arranged the two boulders on either side. Taking a deep breath, he blew dust over the pile. Partially visible under the stone and dust, the vase appeared aged.

185

"Beautiful. Not too obvious yet still findable." Sherry laughed.

Marty's voice echoed from the entrance. "Micah says they are on their way. Places, everyone."

Arnie led Sherry to the back. "You're the last defense for Letitia's home," he whispered. Sherry looked for the wooden door but all she saw was a stone slab wedged between two stalagmites. *Some joke*, she thought. She looked for Arnie but he was gone. She leaned back against the stone finding the surface wooden to the touch.

More illusion, she mentally smacked her forehead. Staring in the dim light, she saw the door. *Ooops.* She concentrated on the door, wishing it to become stone again. As full dark descended, she saw the grain disappear and the rough stone surface take its place. *It wasn't so hard. Aunt Agatha will be pleased.* She crouched down.

An arm draped over her shoulder. She twisted to look, slipping onto the ground.

Nick settled beside her, his finger on his lips. "Thought you'd like company to watch the fun."

Voices echoed from the tunnel.

***

"So, the kids were right." Dawson shook his flashlight but it remained dark. The flashlight in Nate's hand flickered on and off for a few steps then failed. He pulled a flare from his backpack and struck it on the rock wall. The light exploded. The men covered their eyes and blinked against the light blindness. Dawson knocked it from his hand and stomped on it.

"Idiot!" He turned on Nate. "Just 'cause you're young, doesn't mean you have to be stupid." Nate cringed, backing away. Dawson took a deep breath. "Okay, everyone ready?"

186

Sam and Gene lit the kerosene lanterns. Sam handed one to Nate. Dawson held his high above his head and walked on down the tunnel. Each man followed suit to not lose what little vision they had.

Gene yelped and jumped back, his lantern shaking violently. "Something ran across my foot!" He danced in place, swinging his lantern close to the ground.

"Damn it, Gene. It's a cave. There may be creatures in here. Most likely bats if there is another entrance. As fresh as the air is, there is one." Dawson stalked on.

"Bats don't run on the ground." Gene mumbled. He held up his lantern and followed the boss. "Yikes, there is it again." He jumped back against the wall dropping his lantern. The kerosene spilled out on the floor. Eric and Nate stepped around the flaming puddle and pushed on down the tunnel.

"Gene, get a grip. Go on ahead. You've got enough light from my lantern." Sam nudged him, setting him stumbling down the tunnel.

"Whatcha' doin'?" The sweet voice came from behind Sam.

"Shit!" Sam swung around. "How'd you get down here?" He peered down the tunnel, moving his lantern to illuminate the walls. A rat stared back at him. "Gene, found your foot stomper. It's a rat."

Gene edged up behind him, looking over his shoulder. "Rat, my ass! It's a small dog. Look at the size."

"Come on, Norway rats get up to eighteen inches long not counting the tail."

Gene punched him in the shoulder. "Enough with the lecture. I'd rather get away from it." He hurried down the tunnel after the disappearing lights.

Sam straightened up.

"I said, whatcha' doin'?"

Sam swung around, nearly tripping over Garnet. "I knew you were here. Now go away before you get hurt." Garnet avoided his grasp, slipping under his arm and running after Gene. Sam hurried behind her but when he caught up to Gene, the rat hung from Gene's pant leg. Gene slapped and danced to knock it off.

"Where'd the girl go?" Sam demanded. He swung the lantern at the rat.

"Damn it, Sam. I've got a rat on my leg. I didn't see any girl." Gene hopped one more time and the rat scrambled back down the tunnel.

"The little girl from the zoo. I was just talking to her and she ran this way."

Gene shook his head. "Sam, seriously, I only saw the rat."

A scream ended the conversation. Sam and Gene ran down the tunnel and skidded to a stop just inside the large cavern. Eric stood stock still, his lantern shaking in time with his hand.

"It's got me. It's got me." He said over and over.

Sam touched his shoulder, eliciting a whimper. "Eric, buddy. What's got you?"

"My ankle. It's got my ankle."

Sam leaned down but could not see any restriction on Eric's ankle. He straightened, patting Eric on the shoulder. "It must have been the rat we scared up back there. But it's gone now." He pushed Eric to get him moving.

Eric stumbled forward, nearly falling as his foot stayed in place. "No, man, it's still got my ankle." Sam leaned over again. A stone hand grasped Eric's ankle ... a hand protruding from the solid rock wall.

Sam tapped it with his finger. A second hand stuck out. Sam froze. Arnie let Eric's ankle go and pulled himself from the wall, rising first to his knees then standing to tower over the three men. He scowled at them.

Gene shrieked and ran back down the tunnel toward the dock. Eric's eyes ran from the floor up the heavily muscled man looming over him. He gulped several times then followed Gene at a dead run. Sam took breath to stop them but when he looked back at Arnie, the wall was blank and smooth. Sam ran towards Dawson.

"Dawson, we've got some serious trouble here." Sam skidded to a stop nearly tumbling into the pool. "Dawson, where are you?"

"What the hell, Sam? I'm right here." Dawson stepped out from behind a massive stalagmite, its tip nearly meeting the stalactite dripping water in a slow cadence. "Where's Gene?" He looked around. "And Eric. I told him to stay by the entrance. What the—"

"There're creatures here," Sam tried to still the shaking in his voice. "One just came right out from … the wall." He pointed to the alcove by the entrance.

"Out from solid rock?" Dawson grabbed Sam by the collar and hauled him close. "No more ghost stories. There isn't anything there." He shoved Sam against the wall. "Get your wits about you."

"Mr. Hughes?" Nate's voice echoed. "I found something. Over here." Nate waved his lantern.

Dawson dropped Sam. His knees buckled. He slid down until he realized he was seated part way to the floor, the bench feeling like two hands on his buttocks. Sam jumped up. The hands extended from the rock outcropping. They gave him a thumbs-up and pulled back into the wall.

His mouth too dry to call out, Sam looked around for Dawson. Dawson's lantern bobbed along the pool's edge coming toward him. In the reflected light, Sam saw movement in the water—large bodies with long hair floating toward the surface.

"Dr. Ramhill says they're *teppichs*." Garnet stepped from behind Sam. "They don't eat meat ... usually." Sam lunged for her. Her form melted from her three-foot height. Thick brown fur sprouted as she disappeared with a squeak. Sam sat down hard, the world spinning around him.

Dawson's light came closer. He nudged Sam with his foot. "Get up, Sam. I don't know what you boys've been smoking but it's seriously affecting your perception." He gestured at Nate. "Here's a young man with guts. Found the artifact on the first try." He kicked Sam. "Get your monitor. Check this out." Sam fumbled in his pack for the device.

"Leave here now." A tall figure covered in a greenish white haze, black orbs rolling in her head, rose from the dark waters. Her white teeth gleamed in the light. Her voice rumbling near sub audible, it raised the hair on their necks.

"I told you go." Her words echoed throughout the cave. She raised both arms swinging them in a wide arc. Christian's quarterstaff connected with Nate's knees. He fell onto the rock floor, tossing the vase at Dawson as he went down. Dawson caught the vase without taking his eyes from the dripping apparition.

The cavern walls glowed green matching her skin and gown, the intensity rising. Three tall figures grew in gloom, towering over the men, the last one appearing sporting wings hovering three feet above its head. Long grey hair twisted and curled slowly around the female's head and shoulders. Great green eyes glowed from the form on her shoulder. The eyes sprang forward, launched at Dawson's head, the wildcat battle cry splitting the air.

190

Dawson dodged, the claws scraping his cheek as the wildcat flew over his shoulder. He swiped at the dripping blood then grabbed Nate by his belt, hauling him to his feet. The two ran down the tunnel.

Sam stared after them. Stunned, he tucked the monitor back into his pack, a normal act in unusual circumstances. The black quarterstaff slammed point down beside him. He threw the pack in the air. Christian, his all-black attire rendering him nearly invisible, snagged it on the quarterstaff, the pack hovering in midair.

Sam's eyes rolled back in his head. He slumped against the wall.

"Christian, it isn't nice to scare the gentleman." Chaszel commented as she folded her wings. Arnie stepped out from the cavern wall, his chest heaving with laughter.

Sherry pushed her way around Madrecita and Greg with Marty and Garnet behind her. She squatted beside Sam and laid her fingers on his neck. "He is out cold but his pulse is good. He'll be alright."

"Micah says both boats are gone. They've left him behind." Garnet patted Sam's head. "He doesn't talk much, but I like him."

"No, Garnet, you can't keep him." Marty sighed. "Jonas is bringing Nick's boat around to the dock. Probably the best way to take him back to town." A splash interrupted him.

Madrecita held out her hand for her husband to pull her from the water. She shook her head, her long hair throwing water in all directions. "My apologies but the makeup makes me itch." Gregariel laughed. He pulled her into a tight hug, his mirth rumbling around the group.

"I'd say we all need a warm meal and a good stiff drink!" Sherry smiled at them. "On the house, naturally. I am certain Nick won't mind." Nick appeared beside her, cradling

191

Miasma in his arms. He nodded, his sharp white teeth gleaming in the gloom.

Christian gathered Sam up and settled him over his shoulder. "One boat won't take us all."

"We'll go the overland route." Greg said. Sherry raised an eyebrow. "Arnie found another entrance just beyond the last stalagmite on the right. It leads out to the hill top. We can walk through the zoo to the subway."

Madrecita hugged Sherry, dripping on her shoulders. "We'll meet you at the bar."

Garnet tugged at Marty's sleeve and inclined her head toward Madrecita. "If big Mother doesn't mind, you may go along." Garnet scampered after Madrecita. "She has the yen to explore. Can't blame her. I did, too, at her age." He offered his arm to Sherry.

"Where's Triss?" Sherry looked around the cavern as the lights began to dim.

"She said she'd put out the lights and go with the trolls." Marty lengthened his stride to move Sherry along.

Chapter Twenty-Four

Celebration at the Waterline Bar

"Gino, keep it coming." Marty held up his empty beer mug. Gino snatched it from him, filled it and slid it along the bar. Pouring another double Scotch, he handed the tray to Micah. At a nod, Micah took it to the far corner.

Nick leaned back on his chair, a wary eye on Sherry as she studied how far her foot was from the two back legs. Vincent chuckled at the two. He held out a glass to Letitia. She sat in the corner, her eyes flicking from face to face in the crowded bar.

She leaned close to whisper in his ear. "Vincent, are you certain I am safe among these people?"

"Of course, my dear. Perfectly." He looked around the bar. "At the table over there are the clan mothers ... Trolls and the Gargoyles. Their husbands are the two testing themselves with arm wrestling at a table. Micah here," Vincent patted Micah on the arm. "Is a fine wererat ... *Rattus intelligencious*. His mother and father—Anastasia and Marty— are close to the beer taps."

Letitia studied every face.

"So, you see, the only person about whom you should have any concern is Christian here," he nodded to Christian on his left. "Because he is a—Owww!" Vincent jumped up. "My tail, Christian. You have big feet."

"My apologies, Professor." Christian leaned over the table closer to Letitia. "What he was about to say, is, despite our previous unfortunate introduction, I hope we can be friends." He offered his hand to her. She stared at it, then at his face and back to his hand.

Nick laughed. "Don't worry, Letitia. Christian's harmless especially when he's been so handily bested in a fight."

Christian shot Nick a withering look. "Didn't fare so well yourself, laddie." Christian jumped as Letitia placed her hand in his. The warm, silky skin teased along his palm.

"Very well then, gentlemen. I find I must place my trust in you."

Sherry choked on her scotch. "I'm not certain I would go that far!"

Vincent laughed at Sherry's outburst. It turned into a guffaw when he looked at Nick's attempt at an innocent face. Letitia stared at him, the corners of her mouth tugging upward until she could contain it no longer. Sherry dabbed at her eyes, tears welling up. Finally, she grabbed her sides and gasped for air.

Jonas appeared from the downstairs tunnel. He looked from face to face. Nick snagged a chair and pulled it to the table. Jonas handed him the keys to the boat.

"Jonas, join us." Nick waved to Gino. "What are you drinking?"

"I don't know. I've never drunk much but sweet wine. Didn't care for it, though."

Gino set a glass before Jonas. "Try this. It's a Manhattan. I wager you'll like it. I can usually tell."

Jonas took a sip. His face flushed but he hummed a moment. "Gino, you're a genius. This is great." Jonas took another sip, a beatific smile on his face.

194

"What's the report on the man from the cave?" Christian looked at Jonas.

"Safely on his way with the others. I left him in a chair in the hotel lobby. He was just coming around. His friends found him and hustled him to the truck. Both trucks left going south toward the city." Jonas sighed, contentment on his face.

"I'm certain the Mayor will be pleased." Nick nodded at Yancy's approach.

Professor Lizzard edged Letitia farther in the corner making room for Yancy's chair. "Letitia, may I introduce our Mayor, Yancy Fairhaven. You've already met his lovely wife, Triss."

Letitia nodded to Yancy. "Yes, she has been most kind."

Yancy smiled. "Welcome to our little town. Triss tells me you'll be quite a wonderful addition to our community. I hope you will be happy here." Micah set a triple dirty martini close to his hand. Picking up the glass, Yancy raised it high. "A toast … to team work, a bright future for the zoo and a new member in our community."

All clinked their glasses around the table.

"Yancy, where is Triss?" Vincent looked around the bar.

"She went up to tell Madam and Granny all about the night's adventures." He smiled. "And I get to fill in the Town Council tomorrow. It'll be my pleasure to explain the project has been cancelled." Staring into his glass, he muttered. "Now what to do about the water system?"

Letitia reached across Christian to touch Yancy's hand. "I believe I may have something to contribute there." She looked at Sherry, who stifled a yawn behind her hand. "Professor Lizzard explained about the brimstone and the *teppich's* affinity to it. The portal I used to escape from Hecate is now closed." Letitia paused, looking down, unable to meet anyone's eye. Lizzard patted her hand. She looked up and smiled at him.

"Which explains why the second readings were lower than the first." Lizzard patted her hand again before reaching for the biscuits.

"The *teppich* are already going back to their own waters since the brimstone is dissipating." Sherry chimed in.

"Yes," Letitia frowned. "I would like to be able to keep a few. They make very good scrub brushes. Perhaps they can help clean up the water system without it needing replacement. From the detritus in their fur, there is an accumulation of limbs and garbage in the system."

Yancy raised his glass again, only a few drops remaining. "That is a grand idea, especially if it doesn't involve more expense."

"Mr. Mayor, it will involve some expense." Sherry's eyes lit up. "To keep the *teppichs* happy and fed properly, we will need watercress ... a large amount. I propose a new pond on zoo property. I'm certain Greg will help me with the project." She nodded toward the troll husband locked in mortal arm combat with Arnie.

"Arnie, no fair turning to stone. Stay flesh and blood!" Greg smacked Arnie across the head with his free hand. Arnie grunted, his grey face turning tan again. He grinned, large incisors shining in the light.

Everyone laughed at the age-old argument.

"As much as I am enjoying the evening ..." Sherry glanced at the group. "I am knackered." The men all stood as she rose from her chair. "Oh, sit and enjoy. My car is just down the street. I am quite capable." She stared at each in turn until one by one, they sat down.

"Letitia, I will call on you in the morning. After the foodstuffs for the animals is safely stowed."

196

"Don't worry, Dr. Sherry." Micah stepped around Sherry to deposit several full plates on the table. "I'll be there to help. And I'll drag Da along as well."

Sherry patted him on the back. She picked up her purse and took the stairs to the street above. Through the high narrow window, Nick and Christian watched her feet drag up the steps.

***

Sherry stepped onto the side walk and, in a few steps, entered the darkness beyond the bar's neon light. At first, her pace reflected her fatigue. Then she realized she was alone on the deserted street. *I didn't realize it was so late.* She listened to her heels clicking on the pavement. The rushing water in the river provided the only other sound. She pulled her keys from her purse.

"Dr. Ramhill." His low voice startled her. She peered into the darkness, her SUV several feet from the nearest light post. His large frame separated from where he had been leaning on the bumper. "I was hoping to have a word with you."

"Mr. Hughes, you startled me. I heard you and your men left town suddenly." She stopped, measuring the distance between them and calculating how far she was from the bar.

"I thought we were on more intimate terms, Sherry." He drew out her name as he took a step forward. "I want to know where the artifact is."

"I don't know what you are talking about." Sherry tensed to run back the way she came.

"I wouldn't do that if I were you. I was a running back in college and have kept in shape." He took another step toward her. "Let's not play games. Somehow you found out what we were really after and had your … friends … hide it. The vase we recovered only had a vague magic veneer … which dissipated quickly once we inadvertently got it damp on the river."

Sherry took one step back. Hughes moved forward. "That haunted house you put together frightened my men. Another reason I wanted this little talk. How did you do it?"

"Do what?" Sherry took another step back.

"Don't be coy, Sherry. It doesn't become you. And you are a lousy liar."

***

Jonas' hand jerked, sending his glass careening across the table. "Trouble." He gasped and rose, turning over his chair. He sprinted for the stairs.

Christian followed, pulling his staff from the umbrella stand just inside the door. Nick bolted from his seat. Gino tossed him the black scabbard before he vaulted up the stairs two at a time. Whipping around the corner, they halted. Jonas stood in the dark street beside Sherry. They faced Hughes. Nick edged to the left while Christian approached quietly from the right. They made no noise and stayed in the shadows.

Nick paused when he felt Hughes turn his gaze on him.

"I see you, barkeep. I haven't survived this long without some inner senses." Hughes chuckled. "Sherry and I were just having a friendly conversation … before her boys arrived." He glared at Jonas and took a step closer.

Christian whistled and tossed the staff to Jonas. Jonas caught it … overbalanced and danced to keep his feet. He swung it point toward Hughes. Hughes bent his knees, his hands assuming a defensive position.

"Now see here." Sherry stamped her foot. "I will not have a street brawl on my watch." She glared at each in turn. "Mr.

Hughes, let me make myself perfectly clear." She stood ramrod straight. *Madam would be proud*, she thought.

"These are *my* people. Your little game hunting so-called artifacts will not be tolerated here. Sometimes, the item you seek is important to the local ecosystem —if not this whole continent—and needs to stay exactly where it is." She took a step toward him, waving Jonas back when he moved with her. She poked Hughes in the chest with her perfectly manicured index finger. "It would be best if you followed *your* boys back to wherever you came from."

Hughes rocked onto his back foot. He laughed. "Sam told me about the wolverine in the zoo. I didn't believe him. But …." He saluted her with two fingers to his forehead. "I think I have met one who takes human form."

He bowed, his hands together over his chest. "Gentlemen, while a good spar would work out the kinks in my back, I don't believe Dr. Ramhill will allow us the privilege. I bid you good night."

"And farewell," Sherry added.

Hughes studied her face. "For now, Sherry. For now." He turned and faded into the shadows.

"Nervy Yank." Joining arms with Nick and Jonas, she smiled at Christian, her fatigue forgotten. "Gentlemen, I believe I've earned another drink … on the house."

Now you've met Sherry, let us introduce her brother Charlie.

From Foxhaven Chronicles: Raven's Eye

Charlie Ramhill's asthmatic MG ran exactly twelve miles over the speed limit. He drummed his fingers on the steering wheel anxious for the drive to be over. *Home.* He'd been making this drive for over a year. *That's the first time I've called it that.*

Humming a melody, he considered a song for the next gig. He yawned, his jaw cracking. *I should have helped them load the equipment. I wish she'd travel with us.* He rolled his shoulders. *Gods, I miss her.*

The remaining miles rolled by in rhythm to the remembered drumbeats—his perfectionist percussive imperative. *Will I ever get this love song finished?* He tried out a melody to fit the words, his rich tenor filling the car.

> I can't help but be amazed
> Finding my joy mirrored in you
> I'm the one who sees the darkling moons
> But now I'm asked to join your luminescent

dance.

He turned into the drive. Snowflakes careened across the windshield. He stopped, peering into the gloom, pale lights in the distance. "Welcome to my demented Oz." He wondered what she was wearing then chuckled, knowing the answer...his shirt her preference over the designer clothes her mother provided, a belated trousseau.

The car coughed, wheezed and died. *Damn it, I'd best keep my daydreams in the boot until I've navigated this gauntlet.* He turned the key, ground the starter motor until the engine caught. Putting it in gear, he edged it between the lilac's bony fingers. He gritted his teeth, staring down the narrow lane dimly illuminated by feeble headlamps,

There, there on the right side. He eased the car down the drive. Glancing up at the security pole, he cursed under his breath. *Light is out again. Niki is here which means his damn cat is, too.*

He glanced at the shifting branches inky black in the falling snow. The wind drove the flakes dancing in swirls along the muddy drive. The underbrush writhed in the gusts.

So where are you, your feline devil? Charlie squinted his eyes. The car rolled, quickening the pace. He hunched his shoulders against the thickening in the air, a pressure from above.

A heavy body slammed onto the hood, darkening the windshield from edge to edge. Leathery wings beat on the slick glass. Claws scrabbled for a purchase.

"What the hell?" Charlie stomped on the brakes, killing the engine. The writhing form slid, claws screeching along the hood, and landed beyond the projected light.

Acrid stench flooded the vents, gagging him. The bitter taste on his tongue recalled memories he thought long forgotten. He coughed, retching, his breath fogging the windshield.

He wiped his gloved hand across the glass, banging his knuckles against the rearview mirror. Through the porthole, he searched for the apparition, scanning in all directions. Seeing nothing, he leaned his forehead on the steering wheel, his knuckles stinging.

I left this horror behind in England. Why...? The question hung unfinished.

Childhood memories, the dark manor house, his relief at being sent to away to school and the dreaded summers at home flooded his mind. He spent many days visiting school chums rather than to be with his father and brother.

He knocked his head on the wheel, then raised his eyes to the road. Stretching his fingers, he wiped his face. "Okay, Ramhill. Be reasonable. This is the Colonies. There is water, a lot, between here and there. You're tired at the best ... and hallucinating at the worst."

He started the car. "Either way, you have to get down this damned drive."

A few feet farther along, a black ball unrolled in the headlights. Pyewacket's deep green eyes shone red in the light, melting snow glistening on his fur. He flicked his paw, flinging mud, and ran his tongue over the pad before limping to the brick wall beside the cast iron gate. He leapt into the darkness beyond.

"Damn it, Pye!" Charlie pounded his fist on the steering wheel, fuming when the windshield fogged over again. "What is the phrase Sami repeats," he said aloud welcoming his own voice in the chaos "Breathe deep, seek peace. What I need most right now, peace." Peace, a foreign concept in the loud music, the crowds, on the road... all the chaotic elements rendering his life how he wanted it.

He cringed at the grinding gears. The car crept through the gate, stopping even with the front steps. Turning the ignition, he realized the car sat on the left side of the drive. Five years in America and he parked on the wrong side. He considered pulling over but his fatigued muscles argued against it...even stronger, his drive to be within the house and into the light.

The driver's door closing punctuated his deep sigh. He searched for the cat while he pulled out his case. *Claws in my knee are not on my agenda.* Inhaling the cold night air, cinnamon and clove sang on his tongue raising his desire for a warm fire and a strong drink. *She always knows when to pour the brandy to be properly warmed. Is Pyewacket her early warning system?*

The first wooden step to the porch groaned. *F sharp*, he mused. He stepped up. *A flat.* He stepped back down, his adrenaline surge waning with the notes. *Hmmm, from the first to the third ... C, and the first, the second ... discordant but possibilities.* Perhaps he was welcome after all, this amusement just for him. He jumped from step to step, playing his offkey hopscotch. Etude des l'Escaliers Avant, he anointed the piece. His unfinished symphony resonated in his head, forcing the darkness behind him.

He turned the brass knob, unlocked as usual. He frowned. Concern for her safety didn't impress her. Touring with the band for weeks at a time, he worried about her alone. Growing up in a household filled with dogs—hunting dogs, herding dogs—the presence meant security. Sami refused a dog along with locking the door. *For a woman so resistant to ever leaving the house, she shows no fear someone might come in.* He chewed his lip, deciding the discussion should wait until after the holidays.

The heavy oak door swung open, warm air wrapping around him. The entry floor and stairway—lustrous red oak and bright mahogany—gleamed in the candlelight. Golden candles flickered in the swirling air. *The color of Sami's hair.* His throat tightened. The wind gusted from behind, battering him aside and setting the flames dancing. He drank in the silence. *Home ... our home ...* the feeling lifting his heart.

Niki's lilting tenor from the kitchen broke the moment. Sami's crystalline laughter responded to Niki's story. The sound swept over him, igniting his jealousy and sending the candlelight spiraling, increasing the RPMs before setting him down hard. Niki always made her laugh—free, full-hearted laughter—so different from her response to him or to his band mates who joined them in this retreat.

4

He drove away his irritation at Niki's easy manner with her. Niki's gift wasn't limited to Sami. The light in Niki's boyish face always sparked a celebration. Niki focused on each equally.

Charlie shrugged off his coat, trying to hang his worry on the coat hook. He found the snifter on the mantle. *The temperature of a woman's skin.* The touch drove the cold from his fingertips. He savored the rich aroma. Anxious to hold Sami in his arms, he paid the entrance requirement with the short moment alone.

She insisted he take a deep breath and appreciate the beauty unveiling before him. At first, the ritual irked him, fueling his concern regarding her obsessive-compulsive behavior. Now, he looked forward to the moment, the fire warming his legs, the brandy burning his throat, quiet all around him. He marveled at his good fortune.

Studying the room, he searched for changes … what she accomplished over the weeks he was away. A wind rose inlay gleamed in the firelight where the floor had been scorched from a long-distant fire. He imagined her slim fingers smoothing the wood, her love caressing him.

Charlie downed the amber liquid and sprinted for the kitchen. He swung around the jam and swept her into his arms, the ladle in her hand clattering to the floor.

"I don't know which feels more welcoming to me, the warmth of this kitchen… or holding you. It's good to be home." Charlie lowered her until her feet touched the floor. Sami pulled his head down and kissed him, long and deep.

"Hmmm, the way I like my brandy." She licked her lips. Blushing, she gazed up at him from under silky bangs. Her amber eyes gleamed with reflected light from the copper pots hanging over the kitchen island.

He buried his face in her hair. This first moment overwhelmed him no matter how many times he arrived.

5

He looked up and met Niki's eye. "I see you are still blowing out the security light like your namesake in that old movie."

Niki's smile grew puckish.

"You just arrive?"

Niki looked away from Charlie's gaze for a moment. "Yeah." He sipped from his glass. "I talked with a guy who owns a club in Baltimore. He has a cancellation on his holiday schedule."

Charlie sighed, torn between excitement at the growing reputation and bone-deep fatigue. "Don't book us until after New Year's." He caught a fleeting frown on Sami's face when she glanced at Niki. Concern clawed at his throat.

"You know New Year's is a big deal in the industry and I'm tracking the record producer who heard you in Boston last week. He's interested but wants to hear the band again before the year's end." Niki dropped a lemon slice into his vodka.

Charlie tracked Niki's hand. *How often is Niki here when the band isn't?* He shook his head. He desperately craved time alone with Sami.

"How was the gig in New York?" Niki's voice pulled Charlie to the present, his weariness crashing down on him.

"Fine. Not a crowd but some music reporter types. Scotty pays attention to those things." Charlie reached for a glass, splashing scotch into the crystal.

Sami snuggled under his arm, running her hand across his chest. "Why don't you go shower? I'll have dinner ready by the time you're done. Mulligan stew. Perfect for you vagabonds."

He spun her in a dance turn and sang out. "I've wined and dined on mulligan stew"

Sami put her hand on Charlie's cheek and sang the refrain, "And that's why the lady is a tramp."

Charlie grabbed her shoulders, staring at her.

"What?" She laughed.

"I've never heard you sing. You have a lovely voice."

Sami's ears reddened. "You inspired me."

Charlie pulled her into a tight embrace, pouring all his love into his kiss. She responded, sending his heart pounding.

Sami pulled free. "About that shower …." She picked up the ladle.

"What?" Charlie chuckled, echoing her earlier question. "Oh, right."

The aroma set his hunger rising but his shoulders craved hot water. He brushed his lips across her forehead. "Be down in a minute. Stew smells wonderful."

The golden candle flames in the hall reminded him of the gift still in his topcoat pocket. He pulled out the ring box and opened it. The faceted amber ring caught the flames, glowing for the only woman who could fill his heart. *I won't wait until Christmas.*

At the threshold to the kitchen, he heard Sami's lowered voice, "Niki, you have to be careful. I told you he would notice if you were here early."

"Sorry, Sami. I had to get here before he arrived. We needed the time."

"I haven't figured out how to explain all this to him." Her tone switched to light teasing, lifting the mood. "And you're a lousy liar."

Charlie froze.

Niki laughed. "Of course, he won't understand." Niki affected a formal British accent. "A certain rigidity in the thinking, you know. Comes from all the stiff upper lip and boarding school training."

"Stop it, Niki. Charlie's very open-minded. But this may be more than even he may accept. I don't know how to tell him."

"The Ramhills have their secrets, too."

"Niki!"

"Sorry. I'll be more careful. What can I do to help with dinner? It smells fantastic."

Leaving the ring box on the hall table, Charlie dragged his bag up the stairs.

Carolyn Houghton

 I admit it. I am a spiritual child of Walter Mitty, James Thurber's character who lived his real life in stories he made up while coping with his every day, humdrum life. I loved to pretend. I still do. Writing about time travel, being a musician, a goofy (but brilliant) member of the English elite, is a wonderful way to spend my time. I hope you'll also find a fine escape as well in the *Foxhaven Chronicles* and, soon to come, *Waterton* series.

When I'm not wandering around in alternate universes, I'm the proud mother of Celia Ann. She looks at the world in quite unusual ways. My children's book, *Celia and The Land of Discouraging Words* is the result of an evening's conversation. The town I lived in for many years provided love and support when one of my family members was seriously hurt. *I love Summer the Best* is my love letter to the town that was more than willing to help.

Music provides the heartbeat in my life. You'll find lyrics in the back of the books that reflect Charlie's love for Sami, and Mac's worries about zombies. You just never know who will have a story to tell in lyrics.

My writing partner has helped me to grow in many ways. It's so wonderful to think about what am I seeing, tasting, smelling, touching and hearing? She reminds me that the world doesn't always center around dialogue. I'm grateful to have her constancy and brilliance in my life.

The Carrolton Writer's Guild has provided wonderful support for my story telling and poetry. I urge you to find a group that will help you to refine your stories.

Contact her at Carolyn.Houghton.Writer@gmail.com or visit on Facebook at Carolyn Houghton, Writer.

Elyse Wheeler, Ph D

Elyse Wheeler spent many summers hidden away in the small library in northern Illinois trying to figure out who she wanted to be. Following in the path of the scientists/physicians in her family, she completed a PhD in Human Physiology and Biophysics and training in medical technology. She led laboratory services in two major medical centers. Along the way, she published several scientific articles and wrote three book chapters. To finish out her career in science, she designed and implemented two programs (BS and MS) in clinical laboratory sciences and retired from education after 15 years' service.

Raising her son and introducing him to Dungeons and Dragons at an early age has kept her fantasy worlds rich and robust. She is now free to pursue writing the stories she always wanted to read (and let's be honest, live.) With her co-author, she is currently writing the second volume in *Foxhaven Chronicles* and editing the companion series *Waterton Zoo*. She is also writing a YA fantasy novel about a young troll girl and a Pegasus colt.

She celebrates the collaboration with her life-long friend and writing partner, Carolyn Houghton with whom the first three novels have taken form.

She lives in Georgia close to her son, Colin, his wife, Dante and two grand-dogs, Sumner and Ashby. The household includes CH, and two rescue cats, Axel and Karmel. She enjoys the company and encouragement of the members of the Carrollton Writers Guild.

Contact her at Elyse.Wheeler.Author@gmail.com or visit on Facebook at Elyse Wheeler Author.

CPSIA information can be obtained
at www.ICGtesting.com
Printed in the USA
LVHW110259041022
729904LV00001B/125